LEXI

___

T GEPHART

T GEPHART

Lexi
By T Gephart

For more information visit:
www.tgephart.com

To everyone who loved Lexi along with me.

ACKNOWLEDGMENTS

I always get emotional when I get to the Thank you part, so many people and I'm worried that the few words I could write won't adequately convey how truly thankful I am but I'll give it a shot.

I wouldn't be able to do this without my family by my side. Gep, Jenna, Liam and Woodley, you are my world.

Thank you to my amazing group of friends who not only support my writing but put up with all my crazy antics- I know I'm intense but you have to admit we have had some amazing adventures.

Thank you to my proof readers and beta readers (Golf, Mini and Juzzie) who make sure I haven't forgotten key words because my mind and my hands operate at two speeds. Feel free to make a dirty reference here if you want, I sure did :)

Thank you to my amazing editor and dear friend Sam who reads, re-reads, edits and reads again my many drafts and isn't scared to challenge me if she's not feeling it.

Thank you to the Blogs and Bloggers who have actively supported me from the start, Forever Me Romance (Tash and

Rose), *Kinky Book Klub* (Helen), *Kelly's Kindle Konfessions* (Kelly) *and Francessca's Romance Reviews* (Francessca) *and Karen Harper* (now with your own blog *A thousands Lives book blog*). You took a chance on me, I will never forget you.

Thank you to my Gian for the amazing cover, as always you take my vision and "kick it up a notch" – Grace your input was integral as well.

Finally thank to all the readers who loved the first book and followed Lexi through her journey. It has been my unbelievable pleasure to tell this story, thank you for allowing me to share it with you.

PREFACE

When I first sat down to write *A Twist of Fate* I never imagined it would be anything more than a story I shared with a select group of friends. In my trademark impulsive fashion I set out to write a book that *we* would enjoy, I had never intended it for larger consumption. It was only after that small group of people had devoured it and insisted that I not only publish it but write another book that I thought maybe it was more than just a "laugh" among friends.

In a complete ninja-stealth-move, I self-pub'd the book with no knowledge of what I was doing - no cover reveal, no blog tour, no teasers, no ARC's (I didn't even know what this was) and no blogs/blogger support. It wasn't about the money so I listed it as free and joked that if 1000 people read my book I would pop the Champagne and toast my success.

Never, and I do mean NEVER, could I have even imagined what would happen next. Readers from all over the world were downloading it, reading it, loving it. I reached that magic 1000 number within a couple of weeks, getting messages from all over Europe, Asia, North and South America telling me how much they loved Lexi and her story. To say I was floored would be an understatement; I was humbled beyond measure to think that something I wrote was in the hands of so many people.

I have since released 3 complete novels and a novella in the Lexi series and have learnt so much about not only self-publishing but about the amazing human spirit as well. It wasn't always peachy; there were people whose intentions and actions were anything but honourable and some who were downright hurtful. Despite this minority of detractors, I was bathed in kindness, generosity and support not only from my family but bloggers, readers and other authors (I still get giddy when I get messages from authors I adore).

So this book, the final in the Lexi series, (which ironically travels back in time) is a free book and will remain so as a constant reminder of the kindness and love I have been shown by the thousands of people who loved the story and wanted a little bit more. It's my thank you for your support, for reading, despite me not being the *hot new thing*, for taking a chance on a nobody who's only goal was to tell a good story with some interesting characters.

I hope over time to connect with as many of you as possible so that I can thank you in person and I will never take what I have been gifted with for granted. Being a storyteller is a privilege, being allowed into your hearts is an honour and something I will never forget.

T xx

PROLOGUE

"YOU KNOW that I love you, right? That's why I'm leaving you, 'cause I love you more than you love me." He hovered above me as I lay motionless on the bed. My body was curled into a ball as my hair fanned messily around my shoulders. I hadn't showered today. I saw no point. I was so tired and I just wanted to sleep. The fact that it was two in the afternoon and I had blown off all of my morning classes was irrelevant. I was drained.

"Ok." I was resigned. I didn't want to fight anymore and I had nothing left to give. If I didn't love him enough then I would never love anyone enough because I was empty. Done. Finished. Spent.

"You shouldn't be surprised Lexi. I mean, you can't really blame me, can you? Look at you? I've tried, but it's impossible to stay with you."

I had no idea why he kept talking. He had clearly made up his mind. We were done. I wanted to cry, to beg him to stay but it wasn't in me. I was a shell, there was nothing left. He had strategically peeled every layer away from me slowly and now I was bare. I had sold out, believed the commercial bullshit about relationships. I had given him everything I had to give and it wasn't enough. I wasn't enough. I was beyond numb, I was cold and so devoid of emotion that I wondered if somewhere in the last couple of weeks I hadn't accidently become a corpse. I sure as hell looked like one.

"Are you going to just lay there?" He huffed in frustration, obviously annoyed that I wasn't crying and clinging to him and telling him my life was over if he walked out the door. If that's what he was expecting, he'd be waiting a while because it wasn't coming. I may be broken but I was never going to beg.

I didn't move. I had no energy and if I had been religious I would have prayed. Prayed for anything other than this emptiness that echoed through my body, my mind and my heart. I hated it. I never wanted to feel it again. I never wanted to love or be loved again. Right now the only thing I hoped for was for it to be over.

"Well I guess I was right then. I was too good for you. Everyone thought it, you know. I tried Lexi, I did. You pushed me to this. Just remember that. This is your doing. I loved you." I heard the words and they should have cut me, like salt on an already festering wound. He was one more person I hadn't been enough for. One more disappointment. One more person to abandon me. One more failure to add to my long list.

My parents would be so proud. I was living up to the legacy that they had created. My birth had been a mistake; a fact they had never let me forget. I was unplanned and unwanted. They had their perfect family unit with the birth of my brother twelve months before me so I was damned because of my birth order, doomed from the start. Of course I hadn't asked to be born, a fact that was conveniently overlooked. No, my dumbass, middle class parents who were too stupid to use birth control spawned me and had then been too heartless to accept the fact they were having another child. There had been no place for me in their life and I had clued on to that fact by the time I hit kindergarten. They fed me, clothed me and educated me and that's where their obligation ended. I saw glimpses of what a nice, normal family could be like; school taught me more than just how to read. I saw other parents with their children, their beaming, pride-filled faces when they greeted them at the end of the day and I kept a secret hope that one day someone could feel that for me.

Despite my secret longing, I had accepted that I was unloveable when *he* walked into my life. His charming smile and attentiveness was like a mythical elixir and I fell hard and deep for the promise of love, acceptance and affection. It was so wonderful at the start, those initial few months where I was his world. While I had lots of friends I was far from being popular, I could count on one hand the ones who would have my back, so to have someone want me like that was a novelty. Sure I had played hard to get at the start, wondering if he was the real deal but it hadn't taken long for him to convince me that he had seen my true worth. It all seemed like such a blur, I don't even remember when it all changed. I spent every minute possible with him, gave up time with my friends, gave him money but most of all I gave myself. I even forgave him when he cheated on me. We had loved each other so we needed to make it work. I don't remember what I did to make him angry, for it all to change, but as much as he loved me and I loved him, he was leaving.

I blinked but the tears didn't come. I guess there was a limit to how much a person could cry and I had reached the quota. Something to cheer about I guess? Small victories.

"Ok... Goodbye." He tried to hide the slight smile that curved at the edges of his mouth as he backed away from me. He knew he had broken me. Whether that had been his plan from the start was irrelevant now. He had worn me down, month after month, and torn from me everything I had thought I was. Strong, independent, beautiful, intelligent. I was none of those things. I was weak. I was clingy. I was ugly. I was dumb. His words. His words that over time had seeped into my brain, burrowed themselves deep like lave ready to hatch and consume me. It was too late. I was infested.

I watched as he slowly moved toward the door, affording me one last chance to beg him to stay. It wasn't happening. I couldn't say anything else. I couldn't do anything else. Why bother? I would always be alone. I belonged alone.

"God you're pathetic," He sighed as he lingered at the door, unable to resist one last blow. I felt nothing, I was dead inside.

He walked through the doorway of my apartment and out of my life, shutting the door behind him. How was that for a metaphor? He was right about one thing, I was pathetic. I stared at the wall opposite me, its blank, dirty surface a reflection of my life. How could I have not noticed how soiled it had become? I didn't even remember what colour it had been originally. Was it white? Yellow? Blue? I raised my hand and ran it along the smoothness of the now grey surface. I wondered how long it would take to clean it, to scrub the years of grime away. I don't know why but I felt a compulsion to clean that wall, to see what was underneath.

Slowly I stretched out from the protective ball I was curled into, my eyes fixed on the dirty wall. I pulled my hair back from my face and secured it into a messy ponytail as I made my way to my kitchen sink. My apartment was small, five steps either way would put you in an entirely different room, which had been handy as I had been able to watch *him* leave without leaving my bed. But that wasn't my concern right now. No. I had a wall to clean. Completely on autopilot, I filled a bucket with warm, soapy water and grabbed a sponge before carrying my bounty back into the bedroom. The water sloshed, threatening to spill over the lip of the bucket as I placed it down on the floor. I slowly lowered the sponge into the warm, bubbly liquid and it felt good across my skin. I squeezed it, wringing out the excess water before placing the sponge flat against the wall. I scrubbed. Hard. I watched as each pass I made across the surface slowly made the wall clean. I couldn't think about him, or my parents, or love. I had a job to do and I didn't care how long it took me. I wouldn't rest until I had scrubbed every single wall in my apartment clean.

1

Roman Renaissance
Twelve months later

THE WARM AFTERNOON sun danced across my exposed,
tanned skin. This was the hottest part of the day, when not only
did the massive fireball in the sky beat down on us unrelent-
ingly, but the concrete beneath our feet could no longer absorb
any more heat, forcing the warmth to spew from its prison
beneath us.

I stretched out my legs as I sat on an upturned crate, my
shorts and tank top barely covered by my white apron. My
head arched back to allow the full strength of the rays to blast
my face. I squinted my eyes shut, unable to suppress my smile
and I breathed in deeply. Rome was everything I had imagined
it to be and more.

I had left Melbourne shortly after completing my degree,
clawing myself back from a broken heart and more importantly
from a broken spirit. It hadn't been easy but anything worth-
while rarely was. Somewhere I had found a glimmer of hope

within myself and I decided that *I* was enough. I didn't need love or to have a boyfriend or even a family. I could be just me, and I could be happy. I met boys and I slept around and I didn't care. It was a wonderful thing, to have that physical fulfilment without the pressure of an emotional attachment. Relationships were for suckers and I was more than ok with mind-blowing sex with no strings. I didn't need to hold myself to standards placed on me by others. I didn't need their approval and if they didn't like my attitude, or me, then that was their issue. I was free and it felt amazing. I wanted to see the world, experience life, after all it was mine for the taking. I had worked it out. Who I was and what I wanted to be, and you know what? I fucking ROCKED!

My asshole parents had tried to shit on my dream of travelling, convinced it was career suicide if I didn't enter the workforce straight after getting the fancy piece of paper that would see every pay cheque I earned for the next few years sapped to pay off my student debt, but I had stopped caring about what they thought. In fact, it made my decision that little bit more delicious, knowing it pissed them off. My smile widened as I remembered getting on that plane with a suitcase I had packed with too many shoes and a ticket with no return date. I had zigzagged my way through countries until I had landed in Rome three months ago with almost zero cash and an inner peace I hadn't known could exist.

My hand wiped away a bead of sweat that trailed along the length of my neck then I twisted my long brown hair into a messy topknot securing it with a hairband I had been wearing around my wrist. I loved this time of the day and I loved the heat.

"*Alessandra, andiamo!* Customers are waiting, *si*? No more day-dreaming." Luigi the portly, bald and very high-strung restaurateur who happened to be my boss called from the doorway of the trattoria. I ambled from my place in the laneway to where he was standing. My ten minute break had evaporated quicker than I had thought.

"*Scusa* Luigi, I'm coming right back." I hoped my warm smile conveyed my apology. He had been so generous, not only providing me a job and three meals a day but also a place to stay. He and his wife's kindness, which initially had me suspicious, was no longer feared. I'd given up on the idea that I would be drugged and sold to some eastern European businessman as a sex slave. After all, I was no virgin, so I doubted my going rate would be very high.

"Lexi," Stefania purred as I entered the main part of the trattoria. "Americano in your section is to die for. Beautiful blue eyes." Mischief danced in her eyes as she craned her neck to see the American tourist sitting at one of my tables, who was currently engaged in an animated conversation with two other men.

He was good looking but certainly not worth dying over. Of course Stefania always had been somewhat dramatic. I couldn't tell the amount of times she almost "died" - it was an everyday occurrence so I really hoped she had her life insurance policy in order.

"He's ok," I shrugged. Stefania was going to end up in a tailspin if I didn't at least ask him to come out with us later. She was such a sucker for foreigners, and I meant that literally. She'd given some Australian a blowjob not two days ago and he had more than appreciated her commitment to international relations.

"Get his number. You can play with us if you like?" Stefania beamed, jutting out her chest a little more as she caught the American staring at her tits.

"He's all yours," I offered, not really up for being an alternate. I never did like sharing my toys. Men were no exception.

Stefania had been trying to entice me into her bed since we met. She was happily playing for both teams and while she appreciated the love of a good woman she preferred if that came with a big throbbing cock as well. Some woman are just plain greedy but she was so adorable you couldn't really hate her.

I sauntered over to their table with a little bit more of a hip sway than was required but hell, a tip is still a tip and I had aspirations of seeing a little more of Europe. Their eyes gleamed with approval as I stood in front of them.

"Good afternoon gentlemen." I pushed the stray lock of hair behind my ear. "Are you ready to order?"

"Well hello there." The blue-eyed American tourist winked, now giving me his full attention. "What a pretty accent. What's your name sweetheart?"

I rolled my eyes at the typical loaded response knowing I wasn't going to need to try too hard to get him to go back to the apartment I shared with Stefania. I was already bored.

"My name is Lexi and thank you." I politely smiled as my eyes grazed over his toned, tanned physique. He was certainly more appealing up close but he didn't set my girlie parts on fire. While I may sleep around, I was still discerning.

"Well Lexi," he lingered over the syllables of my name a little longer than necessary and while I couldn't place his accent, I guessed somewhere in his family tree there was prob-ably a rebel flag flapping from one of the branches. "My name is Josh and this here is Thomas and Shawn." He gestured to the other men sitting around the table. "We are waiting for a friend, perhaps you could keep us company until he gets here." He tilted his head to the empty seat to his right. The other members of his party grinned approvingly at the prospect.

"Nice to meet you." I nodded and smiled, surveying each of the men individually. If I had to hedge a bet, they were all probably in their mid-twenties and judging by their fancy clothes and wrist-wear, they were all playing with Daddy's money. "Shit is that a Patek Phillippe?" The words spilled out of my mouth before I had a chance to sensor as I stared down at the beautifully crafted Swiss masterpiece that glinted in the midday sun. I had only ever seen cheap Balinese knock-offs up close and the one around Josh's tanned wrist was sure as hell not one of those.

"It is!" He grinned as he twisted the watch around his wrist, "You're not looking to rob me, are you?" His eyebrow rose almost as a dare.

"If I was, I wouldn't bother with the watch, it'd be too hard to move without a middle man. I'd go for the bulge in your side pocket instead. Cash doesn't need a fence." I smirked passively while my eyes floated down to his lap.

"How do you know the bulge is my wallet?" Josh flirted as his lips twitched. "Maybe it's something else."

"Well judging by the angle, it's either a wallet or you should be in porn. Are you a contortionist?" I placed my hand on my hip knowing full well the culprit was cash and not an impressive cock.

Thomas and Shawn had no issue laughing at Josh's expense; Josh himself appeared amused by my quick comeback. I could do this all day, quip-pro-quo was my specialty, especially when dealing with bulges. I tried to keep a lid on it with the customers, that shit didn't help when chasing the elusive tip, but every once in a while (ok, more often than that) my mouth had a mind of its own. Meh, sue me.

"Well I was about to apologize for my tardiness but it looks like you have been well and truly amused in my absence." I turned my head towards the new voice behind me.

WOW, was pretty much the first and only word that came into my mind. He was tall. I didn't really know *how* tall, but he was tall enough that even in my highest heels he would still tower over me. Not that I was measuring him, and if I was I'd rather take my ruler to something *other* than his height. His hair was unruly, an I-just-got-out-of-bed mess that accentuated his dark brown eyes. He was rocking a casual business look. Tailored stone-coloured trousers and a crisp white business shirt, with rolled sleeves exposing his smooth tanned skin. Not the kind of tan his American counterparts were sporting, this guy was less an "I've played outside" and more "I am a Mediterranean Demi-God." He was a local, no doubt about it. I watched as his chest muscles flexed underneath the thin fabric of his shirt (no tie and the top two buttons had been left open) and I tried not to make it obvious that I was checking him out as my eyes travelled down his toned body. Yeah, he worked out. No one is that genetically blessed. I casually leaned back onto my heels to get a better look. Nice. Very, very fucking nice.

"Riccardo!" Josh rose from his seat and clasped the Demi-God's hand firmly, he was obviously the "friend" they had been waiting for. "Everything kosher on the home front?"

"Everything is indeed well." The corners of his mouth teased into a smirk. His dark eyes simmered as they raked up and down my body. He made no effort to sit.

"This is Lexi." Josh took the liberty of introducing me, "She was explaining the intricacies of petty theft. Apparently my watch is too much trouble." His smile spread as he elaborated.

"Well then she would be very smart." Riccardo's voice was low, understated but masculine, raw. His English was clearly excellent but his accent teased at each word. He tilted his head towards me in acknowledgement, "Riccardo. Pleasure." I imagined it would be, given half a chance. A pleasure, that is.

"Well you already know I'm Lexi. I dabble in waitressing when I'm not planning international heists. Perhaps I could offer you a beer, just to keep up the ruse?"

Riccardo threw his head back as he laughed, "Yes, a beer would be fantastic. Peroni all around please." He twirled his finger to indicate he was ordering for everyone, not even bothering to check if this suited them. They didn't seem to mind as they watched on passively; obviously a precedent had been set with this group of men.

"I'll get right on that." I watched as Riccardo finally eased himself into his seat before I turned and headed toward the bar. As I sauntered back, pleased that I found someone in the posse I was happy to hook up with, I noticed Stefania was no longer wearing her flirty grin nor batting her eyelashes. Instead she was wide-eyed, panicked and shaking her head. She seemed to have changed her mind about her role as an international sexual ambassador. This was puzzling, Stefania was usually like a heat-seeking missile, once she was locked on it was a tough task to convince her otherwise.

"*Dio mio! Riccardo Cassius?* Lexi, No. Bad News. Not for you. Pick the other guy. The guy in the blue shirt. He's cute. Yes him. Not Riccardo. You can't." Her words rushed out from her lips in a series of whispered, alarmed warnings.

"Who is he and why is he bad news?" I glanced over my shoulder to where Riccardo and his friends were sitting, relaxed and laughing mid conversation.

"Lexi, he is a Cassius. His family owns more of Rome than the Catholic Church. We are talking *big* money. Stockholdings, shipping, they have their fingers in so many pots."

"It's pies. They have their fingers in so many pies."

"Whatever! Pots, pies. They are a force onto themselves. Their family tree can be traced all the way back to the Roman Empire and I don't mean as peasants. Power, Lexi. More than you can imagine. You do not want to mess with them. Riccardo is the youngest son, and from what I know the least scary, but his last name is still the same."

"It's not like I'm going to date him Stefania. You really need to cool it on the dramatics."

"I know I get excited sometimes but this is not one of those times. He is bad. Find someone else to play with."

Stefania's passionate warning did nothing to dissuade me. Hell, it was almost the equivalent to a throw down challenge. I could never resist a dare, especially not one that looked like that.

"Relax Stefania. What's the worst that can happen? I'll have my fun and then I will move on." I picked up the four bottles of beer and placed them on a tray before I walked slowly back to the table.

"Here you go gentlemen." As I leaned over the table placing each bottle carefully in front of each of them, my arm subtly brushed across Riccardo's tanned forearm. He glanced up at me and smiled, a knowing eyebrow peaked in interest.

"So you ready to order or do you need more time?" I popped my hip to the side, holding the empty tray casually in my hand. "I could recommend something if you like?"

"Indeed. What would you recommend?" Riccardo baited, his eyes gleaming with amusement.

"Well, what are you in the mood for? Are you craving anything in particular?" I shamelessly flirted. Yeah, I know it was predictable and probably immature. I had just been told this guy was to be avoided, he was trouble and all I could concentrate on was finding out why. The fact he was so goddamn good looking just made it easier. It's not like I was planning on sleeping with him. Ok, given the chance I would probably sleep with him. I didn't care if people labelled me a whore, I'd been with one guy for two fucking years and all he did was break me, I'll take being a happy whore any day of the week.

Josh, Thomas and Shawn looked on with interest, taking

swigs of their beers as they waited to see how their friend was going to "handle" me. If Josh, who initially showed interest, was pissed that my flirtations were not directed at him he was wearing one hell of a poker face. Or perhaps in this group there was a pecking order?

"I'm feeling adventurous Lexi." His lips twitched as he spoke my name. "Something spicy perhaps. Why don't you choose and surprise me?"

"You might not like what I choose."

"A risk I'm willing to take." Riccardo leaned back into his chair, relaxed and in complete control. He was clearly enjoying himself and despite his self-assured arrogance, he didn't seem cocky. It was enticing but more than that, it was hot.

"Suit yourself." I shrugged, not willing to tip my hand just yet. I could play it cool too. I shifted my attention to the other faces who were animatedly watching our little display. "What about you guys? You want to play menu roulette as well?"

"Oh hell no," Josh laughed. "I don't like to gamble with my food. I'll take the veal scaloppini." He winked as he handed me back the menu.

"I'll take the Ossobuco, I could eat the ass out of a cow." Thomas volunteered as he passed me his menu.

"And I'm tossing up between the Fettuccini Carbonara or this thing called the Coda alla Vacc-in-ara?" Shawn stumbled around the pronunciation.

"Do you know what that is?" I smirked assuming he had no idea what he was ordering. Riccardo laughed, allowing me the honour of explaining.

"Ummmm some kind of meat? " Shawn's eyebrows knitted. "Beef?"

"Oxtail." I smiled, "It's an acquired taste."

Shawn screwed up his face, "Ewww, why do you Italians got to complicate shit?" He playfully shoved Riccardo's shoulder before turning his attention to me. "Yeah, I'm going to go with the pasta instead."

"All good!" His expression had already told me that he would be forgoing the culinary exploration for a safer choice. Judging by the rest of the table's reaction I'm guessing the closest these Americans had gotten to Italian cuisine was at *The Olive Garden.*

As I recited their orders, Riccardo watched my mouth roll through the Italian intonation. Stefania had been helping me perfect my accent while I hooked her up with English. It was mutually beneficial.

He gave me a curt nod acknowledging I hadn't fucked up their order despite not writing it down and I turned and headed to the kitchen.

Stefania watched me as I wrote up the order on a docket, making my choice for Riccardo's meal and handing it to the head chef.

"*Pasta all'arrabbiata?* Lexi, that stuff is not for the weak hearted. You trying to turn him off?" Clearly she did not appreciate my choice or my humour.

"The expression is not for the *faint* hearted, not weak, and he asked for something spicy. I picked the spiciest dish on the menu." I casually chewed on the end of the pen.

"You're crazy. You're messing with him. A Cassius. You have totally lost your brain." Stefania tapped her head dramatically, her wide eyes and frown illustrating she wasn't the least bit impressed. It amused me that she was so concerned.

"It's lost your *mind.* And you worry too much. *Ho tutto sotto controllo.*" My attempt to tell her "I've got this" in both English and Italian did little to appease her as her eyes widened further and she paled to the same shade as the bistro tablecloths.

"You speak Italian very well for an Australian, your accent is impressive." Riccardo whispered into my ear.

I spun around quickly, accidently knocking over a basket of lemons that were decorating the bar. "Shit, don't you know it's rude to sneak up on people?" I watched the lemons tumble to the floor, not willing to get on my knees in front of him - not in this setting at least.

"I'm sorry. I didn't realize I was sneaking. You seemed rather engrossed in your conversation with your charming friend." He gestured to Stefania who was still standing silently.

"Stefania. Her name is Stefania." I offered when it became clear she was still working on her *Madame Tussauds* impression.

"*Piacere Stefania.*" Riccardo tipped his head and smiled. I almost expected him to do the whole kiss-the-hand thing but thankfully he didn't.

"*Signore Cassius.*" She nodded back, unable to offer any more than his name for a greeting. "I need to get back to my tables." Stefania nervously shuffled away from the bar giving me a heated stare which translated into "don't forget what I told you."

"Your friend seemed to be in a hurry." He mused as he watched Stefania leave like the bar was on fire.

"She's intimidated by the fact that apparently your family are God or the Devil. Jury is still out." I didn't know how much he had heard but I was making no attempt to hide the fact we were talking about him.

"What about you? Is this what you believe?" Riccardo dipped his head to meet my eyes. I felt them penetrate me, like he was slowly stripping my clothes off and licking my bare skin.

"I don't believe in God or the Devil." I snapped, not willing to give him the upper hand. I'm sure that while I had started this game, he was more willing to ante up.

"So what is it that you know about my family? Perhaps I could clear up any misinformation." His eyes never left mine as his mouth twitched. I could tell he was fighting a smile.

"I don't judge people by their last name, I make my assessments by their character and their actions." As much as we were playing with each other, this was completely true. One thing the defective, unsupportive horde that I shared a surname with had taught me was you don't define yourself by your family. I sure as hell didn't want to be attached to them and I was willing to pay someone else the same courtesy.

"So young and yet so wise." He moved closer and whispered in my ear, "And what have you assessed about me thus far?"

"I haven't had enough time to make that call," I lied as I pulled back slightly, my face inches away from his. I didn't give a toss who his family was or what they did but what I did know was that I wanted to sleep with him and find out if his smouldering sexiness translated into the amazing sex I hoped it would. I'd been fooled before but something told me that this guy had the goods to back up the ego.

"Well then this is a situation that requires attention, no? Perhaps an evening in my company so you can accurately make this judgement?" He made no effort to move away, his head tilted to the side to gauge my reaction.

"Are you asking me out?" The question slipped out of my mouth involuntarily. I really needed to learn to filter better.

"Yes, I am." He didn't hesitate as his lips spread into a smile.

"And if I say no?" I teased, biting my lip wondering if he was going to make me an offer "I couldn't refuse" a-la *Godfather*. Not that there was anything even slightly mobster about Riccardo, other than that he was Italian, but the whole "family" thing conjured up images of violin cases and Marlon Brando.

"Then I shall enjoy my lunch and be on my way, but I think you want to say yes." He was cocky but still polite, an interesting mix which only made me want to sleep with him more. Yep, he was right. I was going to say yes. I would probably say yes to anything he suggested as long as he kept looking at me like that with those dark expressive eyes.

"Fine, I'll go out with you. Purely in the interest of an informed decision as to whether or not you are good or evil." I tried to play it off like I wasn't the least bit impressed and was merely going out with him as a favour.

"Wonderful, I shall call for you at eight. Where are you residing?" While he spoke English with clarity and perfect understanding, his word-use threw me. It was overly proper and not the kind of language I expected someone in their mid twenties would use. He sounded almost regal.

"I'll meet you somewhere. Nothing personal but I don't accept rides from men I don't know." There was no way I was breaking my carnal rule of always having an exit strategy, even for this guy. I didn't do the whole pick-me-up shit. I found my own way there and back so that any time I wanted to bail I could be gone without relying on anyone. It was a deep seeded need for control that I refuse to give up. It was better this way.

"None taken. Meet me at *Piazza Navona*, you know it? There is a big fountain there, the Fountain of the Four Rivers." If he was fazed by my refusal of a ride, he wasn't showing it.

"I know it, *Fontana dei Quattro Fiumi*." I nodded, knowing exactly where that was. It was actually one of my favourite parts of Rome. The fountain was spectacular with the square surrounding it housing some of the most amazing eateries and bars.

"Your Italian is quite remarkable. I'm rarely impressed but your command of my language is enchanting."

"I'm not just a waitress Riccardo, I have other talents." It was my turn to be cocky; I could feel the air around us thicken.

"Alessandra, food is getting cold." Luigi hollered from the kitchen, breaking the tension.

"I shall let you get back to work. We shall revisit this conversation tonight." Riccardo looked over my shoulder at a flustered Luigi who had emerged from the kitchen.

"Yep, see you at 8." I watched as he turned and walked back to his table. I couldn't stop my eyes from moving down his body assessingly. Nice ass - yeah I was going to be sleeping with him, it was just a matter of when.

2

Dancing with the Devil

THE REST of my shift passed fairly uneventfully. Stefania had brought Riccardo's table another round of beers while he and I had been deep in conversation at the bar and she had managed to secure a date with Josh. In the end she hadn't needed my help, which was handy because I had totally forgotten that had been my objective from the start. She, of course, didn't have the same control issues I did but still insisted he meet her at the trattoria rather than our apartment which was not even a block away. Smart not to let them know where we actually lived, at least not until we got to know them better.

Despite Riccardo's interest in me he was respectful when I brought them their meals and even complimented my menu choice for him. Obviously the "spice factor" was not an issue for him as he devoured the pasta with enthusiasm. Either that or he had more game than I gave him credit for.

They left shortly after, leaving a tip that was generous but not obscene or inappropriate. Guess they weren't as "showy" as I had first pegged them. Interesting.

"Are you sure you don't mind me taking your car? I can take a taxi." I finished applying my make up while Stefania exited the shower. She had no qualms about being nude around me, it was European thing so I just went with it.

"Of course not. It is silly for you to take a taxi when my car is right here. Just make sure you keep up with the flow of traffic. You know the rules are just show, drivers take no notice of them." Stefania towelled off her hair as I took one final look in the mirror.

"Yes, I'm aware of the insanity of this city's drivers. I'll do my best not to piss anyone off by doing something as stupid as following the road rules." I smirked as I left the bathroom.

I slipped on my black heels as I grabbed my clutch, hopping to the door to grab the keys to Stefania's Fiat Cinquecento. The car was basically a box on wheels but it was convenient and ran on vapours, so it was the perfect get around for her. She would happily let me borrow it whenever I needed, Stefania was cool like that.

"*Ciao Stefania*, see you later." I called out from the front door, pausing at the threshold.

"*Ciao Lexi*. Be careful, he is not someone to misjudge." She poked her head out from the bathroom, the concern evident on her face.

"I've got this." I waved and stepped into the hallway, closing the door behind me. One night, maybe two? What was the harm? I was going into this with my eyes open, I was not some stupid girl who needed saving.

The drive to Piazza Navona was thrilling. Threading through narrow streets and dodging speeding cars was more of an adventure than any other mundane method of travel.

I managed to squeeze the tiny car into a park on one of the

side streets not far from the square. The night air was still warm as my heels clicked along the footpath. I had chosen a tight, lace mini dress that clung to my curves. It was black and from a nobody local designer but I loved it. It had cost me next to nothing but made me feel like a million bucks.

I reached the fountain just before eight and took in the magic of the square at dusk. It was breathtaking. People buzzed around, nattering in various languages as the sun started to set, making the sky explode in a sea of bright hues.

"You're looking beautiful," Riccardo whispered in my ear. I hadn't heard his approach as he stood behind me.

I turned slowly to face him, intoxicated by the vibrancy of the evening. "*Grazie.*" I smiled as I took him in as a part of the landscape. He looked flawless in a pale blue, linen suit with another tie-less white shirt featuring underneath.

His dark brown eyes danced with mischief as he took my hand, "And punctual. Deadly combination."

"I hate being late. It makes me crazy." I volunteered, glad he too had been on time. It really did make me crazy, although in this setting, I could have probably tolerated it more than usual.

"A trait we share. I'm interested to see what else we have in common." Riccardo pulled me gently away from the fountain and along the people-filled path.

"So did you have particular plans for this evening other than trying to convince me of your virtue?" This was a genuine concern. He seemed so calculated and controlled I found it hard to believe that he didn't have a minute-by-minute itinerary.

"I'm not trying to convince you of anything," he crooned. "So tell me, what is your real name? Lexi is short for something, yes?" Riccardo placed his hand on the small of my back as he continued to lead me along the Piazza.

"Alexandra, but I hate it. Everyone calls me Lexi." Despite what my birth certificate said, I wasn't an Alexandra. I couldn't even connect that name with who I was, it was so foreign. I don't think I've ever been an *Alexandra* except when my father or mother decided they needed to use it when I was in trouble. Saying the name I despised was almost as bad as whatever punishment they were going to dish out. It pissed me off and they knew it.

"Why would you hate such a beautiful name?" Riccardo stopped short, his brow scrunched in confusion like someone had admitted they didn't like ice cream.

"Because it's a name that I can't identify with. It's strange but I'm not her. I'm Lexi. I can't explain it and I know I'm probably coming across as a lunatic but it just feels like we're talking about someone else, not me." I shrugged, not able to offer a more intelligible explanation. I didn't have anything personal against the name, it just wasn't mine.

"Then I shall call you Alexia. You are too intriguing to be simply Lexi." Riccardo spun his own variation of my name without asking my permission. The way he said it sounded so alluring, I really didn't care what he called me as long as it *wasn't* Alexandra.

"I thought I was supposed be finding out more about you, not volunteering useless information about myself." Useless information is all he was really going to get from me. Pretty much all any man got from me. They unfortunately had to wear the sins of the *boyfriend* past which meant the real Lexi was buried deep and all they ever were going to get was surface stuff.

"No information is ever useless, especially not when it is about a beautiful woman." I couldn't tell if it was a line or if he was serious but his intention to find out more about me was clear. It seemed like I wasn't the only one on a fact-finding mission, apparently Riccardo had intel-gathering on his agenda as well.

"You're avoiding." Not willing to go back and forth any longer, I called him on the fact that other than his name I knew nothing about him or his mysterious family.

Riccardo smiled broadly, "Let's get something to eat and I will tell you everything you want to know."

I nodded as we continued walking along the Piazza until we came to a small bistro. It was plain in its appearance. Tiny wooden tables covered in red and white checked tablecloths and simple high-backed wooden chairs littered the outdoor space. Wine glasses and cutlery sat at the ready, while home-made candles burned brightly in old mason jars providing the only source of illumination. It was understated and quaint and not at all the kind of place I expected Riccardo to know about, let alone frequent. Not that I was stereotyping, ok so maybe I was stereotyping, but I would have thought *Il Convivio di Trolanai* was more his speed. Not that I had ever eaten there because despite its outstanding reputation and my desire to enjoy the finer things, my meagre salary and tips were not sufficient enough to allow it. Beside I got to eat for free where I worked so paying for it just felt like wasted money to me.

An elderly man who must have been about eighty emerged from a narrow, bricked archway which I assumed lead to the inside of the bistro. His face was weathered but kind and it lit up when he saw us. He enthusiastically shuffled toward us as fast his fragile frame would carry him.

"*Ciao Riccardo.*" He greeted Riccardo with a warm hand-shake before launching into a rapid fire Italian dialogue I had no hope of deciphering. I think I heard my name in there at some point but couldn't be too sure and to be honest I'd be guessing, lost in a maze of lilted vowels and hand gestures.

"S-it, s-it." The old man insisted, pulling out a chair before I registered he was actually talking to me.

"Giorgio owns this establishment." Riccardo explained, "They serve the best pizza in all of Rome."

"*Grazie Giorgio.*" I extended my hand and we exchanged a polite handshake before I lowered myself into the chair.

More jumbled foreign words I didn't understand, followed with Giorgio tapping Riccardo on the back before he shuffled back through the doorway and Riccardo slid into his seat opposite me.

"Interesting man. Though you would think at his age he should be kicking back a little more and not working so hard." I lifted the single paged menu and glanced over the beautiful script that graced the thick parchment. Hand-written in stunning calligraphy, I found myself more interested in the sweeping penmanship rather that the food it was advertising.

"Alexia, he loves his work. It's what keeps him young. He lives to feed people, to see their joy through his food. He would sooner die than retire." Riccardo didn't even bother to look at the menu, refusing to take his eyes off me.

"So you come here a lot? Part of your repertoire to charm unsuspecting women into thinking you are just a regular guy?" I wouldn't be surprised if he had scanned the yellow pages (or whatever the equivalent is here) for this place in an effort to look more *ordinary*. The old man was a nice touch, I wonder if he had to pay extra for him. Call me cynical.

"Are you charmed?" He raised his eyebrow as the corner of his mouth curled upward.

"Not yet. Sorry." Not that I cared, I finished in my head. It was Riccardo who wanted to set the record straight; I had already decided I wanted to sleep with him. That wasn't to say I wasn't curious as to why he was being cagey.

"Alexia despite what you have been told I *am* a regular guy, but in answer to your question, yes I came here very frequently in the past but this is first time I have been back in a while." He let out a slow breath, I couldn't tell if he was slightly annoyed by my line of questioning or resigned to the fact no one would ever see him as *regular*.

"Why?" It had to be asked right? I mean he couldn't expect me not to. The question was just hanging there and it's not like me to leave shit just hanging.

"Why what?" His eyebrow rose not understanding my question. I thought it was self-explanatory but perhaps something got lost in the translation.

"Why did you stop coming? It's hard to imagine staying away from the best pizza in Rome or was that claim just for Giorgio's benefit?" If he was going to the trouble of concocting a backstory then it should at least be thorough, or if it wasn't a bullshit line then I was *genuinely* curious as to why. It irked me a little that the interest I had originally feigned was now very real. I couldn't help myself, I was an information junkie and I wanted to know more.

"No. I meant it, as you will soon find out for yourself. I was away from Roma for a while, I've just recently returned." Riccardo further explained which also told me a whole lot of nothing.

"Where did you go?" I really wished he would just spill instead of making me drag every tiny little detail out one by one.

"So many questions." Riccardo smirked, "Are you sure you aren't a reporter as well as a waitress?"

"You did say that at dinner you would tell me anything I want to know. We're at dinner so by virtue I can ask anything I like, right? Or was that false advertising?" It's not like I wanted to play Spanish Inquisition but a deal was a deal.

"I was away at university. Boston. In the United States. My

father believed that studying abroad built strength in character and diversity, I just wanted to go as it afforded me the freedom to not live in the shadow of my last name."

"You went to *Harvard*?" My eyes widened in disbelief. While I was sure there were other schools in Boston, something told me that a man with fancy family ties to Caesar wouldn't go to a community college. Ok, so I made up the bit about the ties to Caesar but Stefania had said something about Roman emperors and not being peasants so I was just doing the math. Of course this also explained why he spoke English so perfectly as I was pretty sure communicating proficiently in English is a requirement for attendance.

"You look impressed. I thought you were not so easily charmed?" Riccardo laughed.

"I'm not charmed I've just heard it's a hard school to get into. What did you study?" I wasn't charmed but I was definitely impressed. I knew how prestigious it was to have a qualification with the *other* big H adorning the page, the first big H of course being Hermès, who sadly didn't give out degrees.

"Business. I continued on and completed my MBA." High achiever it seemed. Wasn't only 9% of the applicant pool actually accepted into Harvard Business School for the MBA program? Why I even knew that was puzzling. I really did store too much useless information.

A waiter filled our water glasses while another brought a plate of warm bread with a small dish of olive oil.

"You tear a piece of the bread and then you dip it into the oil." Riccardo demonstrated, taking a piece of bread then dipping it before slowly sliding it into his mouth. I'm not sure if he was trying to be erotic but I could watch that man eat bread all day.

"So you are obviously super smart as well as super rich." I

tore some of the bread, mirroring his action with the oil before placing it in my mouth. It was delicious.

"I'm not rich Alexia, my father is." Riccardo tried in vain to convince me that he didn't have a money tree in the back yard. The fancy suit, nice watch and super expensive education path hinted otherwise.

"Ok. So what car do you drive?" I was guessing a Ferrari; I couldn't see a guy like this tooling around in a Ford Escort and when he told me he was driving a car that was probably worth more than a down payment for a house, we could put the I'm-not-rich-my-father-is bullshit to bed.

"A test or just further information you require?" Yeah, he was onto me but he didn't seem bothered, I assumed he'd driven here so I could just as easily follow him back to his car and find out.

"Call me curious."

"It's an old car actually. An old Mercedes." He dismissed, playing it off like there was nothing else to the story.

"Really? I'm intrigued. Old as in used or old as in classic?" A Mercedes isn't what I would have picked. In Europe they weren't especially unique and frequented the roads as often as Fiats and Volkswagens. Unless I was completely wrong there had to be more to it than an old Mercedes. Maybe it was gold dipped?

"You are very persistent you know that? It's a 1955 Gull-wing, yes it's a classic."

"Yet you aren't rich?" I didn't know enough about cars to know what the fuck a 1955 Gullwing was and what ballpark we were batting in but judging by the smirk on his face it was something special. Something very special.

"It was a graduation gift Alexia. It's not a big deal." Riccardo waved it off like they had given him an engraved pen set. You know the stainless steel Parker ones that come with the matching pencil that everyone seems to get usually from a Grandma or an old Aunty. *That* would be no big deal, not a whole fucking vintage car.

"My graduation gift from my parents was a voucher with an interview coach although I'm pretty sure it's expired by now." I scoffed. Granted I had expected nothing from the assholes and would have preferred $50 in card rather than a voucher for a service I had no intention of using. What kind of fucking qualifications do you even *need* to be an interview coach? How is that even a real job? I thought for sure it was some scam but there is an actual industry of people to prime you for a job interview.

"A practical gift Alexia. Your parents were very thoughtful." Of course Riccardo was being respectful, he didn't know my parents were dumbasses whom I didn't care about. Not that I would be clarifying that titbit of information. Some things were better left unsaid.

"You want to swap me your classic Mercedes for my expired voucher?" I laughed, pretty sure the answer would be a HELL NO.

Riccardo didn't even bother to hide his amusement. "As tempting as that the offer is, I'm going to have to decline."

A waiter refilled our water glasses and asked if we were ready to order. Riccardo and I had been volleying back and forth so much that I had completely forgotten I was supposed to be deciding what I was going eat. It had been a while since a "date" had been this interesting. Usually I just saw it as a prelude to getting a guy into bed, foreplay, but with him it was different. I was actually enjoying both being here and the conversation.

Riccardo smiled as he conversed with the waiter in Italian, the words once again too fast for me to keep up with, but I assumed it was his dinner order. The waiter nodded as he gently took Riccardo's menu before removing the menu sitting on the table in front of me.

"I haven't decided yet." I stared at the waiter, confused as he made no effort to listen and he left the table. Rude!

"I took the liberty of ordering for you. I thought it was only fair since you decided my lunch, I'd like the pleasure of deciding your dinner."

"But that had been your choice." I tried not to explode over the fact he hadn't bothered to ask permission and wondered if this was payback. "You didn't even ask what I like."

"Relax Alexia, it's just pizza and wine. I promise you will like it. If I'm wrong then we will get you something else." Riccardo reasoned as he twirled his empty wine glass casually. He wasn't even the slightest bit concerned. Bastard.

"I hate fish on my pizza." I huffed, not sure if it was the possibility of seafood polluting my pizza that was upsetting me or the loss of control.

"I promise there is no fish." Riccardo laughed as he relaxed into his seat.

"Seriously if I see a rogue anchovy anywhere on the surface I'll probably flip out. Consider yourself warned." I wasn't kidding, those slippery, fishy motherfuckers made me gag just looking at them. I should have paid more attention to the menu. Damn it. I was acting childishly and I knew it, and yet I couldn't stop.

"Noted." He smirked.

3

One Wild Night

THE WINE ARRIVED and surprisingly it was a sparkling white instead of the red I had anticipated given that it seemed most Italians drank red with every thing. Riccardo explained to me that while the pairing might seem odd the freshness of the pinot grigo grapes was actually better suited to our meal than a full-bodied red. While secretly I was relived (I had a strong dislike for red wine) I wasn't going to give him any credit just yet.

The wine was delicious, light and easy to drink and, as Riccardo had promised, perfectly matched our pizza. Luckily for him while it was piled with an assortment of fresh produce there were no anchovies. Crisis averted.

We chatted while we ate and he told me about his time in America. The three guys who had been with him at the trattoria had been his classmates. The four of them had grown close as they navigated the difficulties of college together and had become firm friends. It had been decided sometime during their freshman year that they would spend a summer in Rome (no doubt after being told how amazing it was by Riccardo - not that he had to lie, it *was* amazing), and so like a corny coming of age movie a pledge was made. Of course an offer to visit Rome would be hard to turn down but the reality of the situation was a little different. Studying and making good grades had taken priority and when summer breaks had finally arrived the boys inevitably either went home or spent their vacation time with girlfriends. It had taken until their graduation for the four of them to coordinate themselves and make good on their promise. I guess each of them had realized it was a now or never kind of time.

As the conversation continued, the pizza, like the wine, quickly disappeared. Although my guarded exterior was still locked firmly in place, my inhibitions soon departed with the introduction of a second bottle. So when he asked me to dance with him, despite the lack of music or a dance floor, I agreed.

He pulled me tightly against his body as he moved us around the tables of amused dinners. They grinned politely and then returned to their meals like we were of no consequence to them. My body was liquid as I allowed him to move it however he saw fit. My hands roamed up the large expanse of his back and I couldn't help myself as I playfully licked his neck. He stopped as my mouth made contact with his skin and reluctantly led me back to our table. I was slightly confused and wondering if I had misread his interest until he pulled out his wallet and placed a number of notes on the table without out bothering to ask for the bill. I guessed that the fanned collection of Euro would more than cover it. I hadn't misread anything; he was feeling the heat too. He nodded to the wait staff as he guided me back through the square, his arm around my waist.

I struggled to maintain my balance wearing heels on the uneven paved road, I'm sure the alcohol hadn't helped my cause with gravity either but it was a little late in the game to be worrying about that.

I lost my sense of direction as we turned down a dim alley. The bright lights of the Piazza provided just enough of a latent glow so that we weren't in total darkness. Not good Lexi. You need to be able to maintain your exit strategy.

Riccardo stopped walking as his hands pulled me against his body in the same way it had been while we were dancing. My body swayed at the sudden movement as his lips came crushing down on mine. My lips parted, allowing him to slip in his tongue. One of us moaned and I couldn't be sure it wasn't me as our kiss deepened.

"Why are you kissing me in the dark?" I panted as my hands moved up his torso.

"I hadn't intended to, I just couldn't wait any longer." His lips brushed along my chin before finding my mouth again.

"So where were you taking me?" I struggled to get the words out in between kisses.

"Dessert." Kiss. "Gelato." Kiss. "A small place." Kiss. "Near by." The fragmented words were disrupted as his lips covered mine, his tongue exploring my mouth.

"Fuck dessert." I moaned into his mouth as I pulled him closer to me, I felt the evidence of his arousal pushing against the fabric of his trousers as I grinded against him.

Riccardo groaned as he hooked one of my legs against his hip and rocked against me. My bare skin tingled as his fingers gripped my thigh. I moved against him to create more friction, his hardness hitting me in the perfect spot.

"Ah," I moaned as my back arched, clawing at his shirt. Coming in a dark alleyway hadn't been my plan for tonight but I was willing to adapt, especially when it felt this good.

"I know I shouldn't be asking this Alexia," he whispered in my ear, "but I want to spend the night with you."

"Then stop talking and take me to bed." I breathed into his ear wondering how long it would take to get somewhere, to get naked and get him into me.

"You're sure that's what you want Alexia? This hadn't been my intention."

"Yes, it's what I want." I rubbed my already over sensitised body against him. "Is your place far?" I was hoping like hell he would say we were actually making out on his doorstep.

"There's a hotel. Close." His mouth moved to my neck and then swirled along the swells of my breasts.

"Ok." I murmured, slightly disappointed that I was going to have to wait. Delayed gratification was bullshit.

"I'm going to set you down Alexia," Riccardo moved his mouth back up against my throat, "then it's just a few streets to the right."

"Ok," I repeated trying to convince myself that dark alley sex would be the wrong move here. I have to admit, the debate in my head wasn't going well and had Riccardo suggested it, I wouldn't have thought twice about getting on board. Both literally *and* figuratively.

"Alexia, we need to walk, *bella*." He gently lowered my leg to the floor as my hands refused to let go of his shirt.

"Right, walking." I pulled my hands from his body, ignoring the screaming protest from between my legs. Did I mention how bad I was at waiting?

We ambled through the laneway and made it to the slightly larger street. Riccardo's hands were restless against my body as we edged closer to the hotel, which had finally come into view.

If I hadn't known any better I would have just assumed it was someone's house. As with most things in this city, they were either over the top ostentatious or so understated that they were almost overlooked. The latter was applicable in the present case. It was a plain white brick building with a large archway. Got to hand it to those Romans, they certainly loved a theme and archways were a serious trend. A thick brass name-plate, no larger than the width of a brick, advertised the name of the hotel with a small number 8 above it. That's it. No happy *vacancy* sign in neon outside or a placard displaying the hotel's address or contact details. I would have walked past it without giving it a second glance. I guess they subscribed to the slightly arrogant school of thought that if you weren't smart enough to work it out then you didn't deserve the room.

"Reception is upstairs." Riccardo guided me through the threshold of the archway and directed me to the steep narrow stairs. The sound of my heels reverberated through the passageway as we climbed, Riccardo's hand pressed gently at the base of my spine.

Riccardo gave me a knowing smile, silently asking me to wait as he approached the lady behind wooden reception counter. With the exchange of a credit card and a signature, a key was handed over and we were climbing more stairs to where our room was on the third floor.

It had only taken a minute after opening the door to our room for me to push Riccardo's jacket off and tear his shirt from his body. What was underneath was just as impressive as I had imagined. Toned muscles tensed as my tongue trailed along his chest, his mouth parting as I flicked my tongue across his nipple.

"Alexia. Bed." He ordered as he lifted me off of the floor and wrapped my legs around his waist and walked us toward the bed.

He reached down with one hand and ripped the bedspread from the mattress, tossing it to the floor, leaving the sheets exposed. My mouth hungered for his as my hands raked through his dark wavy hair. He toed off his shoes as he walked through the room, pulling off his socks one at a time, one handed while balancing me in his arms. I could feel his muscles flex around me, as he maneuvered me with what seemed like no effort.

He half threw/half lowered me onto the bed in a desperate rush and then covered my body with his, allowing his hands to sweep up and down my naked legs. I kicked off my shoes as I fumbled with the button on his pants.

As he pressed against me, my legs opened to allow him to settle in between them. I had managed to undo the button and slide down the zip of his pants but my hands were pinned by Riccardo making it impossible for me to strip them off him.

Riccardo rose off of me and flipped me onto my belly so quickly I let out an involuntary squeal.

"I'm going to unzip you." He whispered into my ear as he pressed his hard cock against my back. I felt him tug at my zipper before the cool air hit my exposed skin. His lips kissed up toward my neck as he pushed my dress from my shoulders.

I took advantage of the fact that he was distracted to wiggle out of my dress and spin around onto my back. My hands violently yanked at the pants he was still wearing despite me un-buttoning and un-zipping them two minutes ago. If they had any decency they would have just fallen off, not that it mattered now as they lay in a crumpled mess with my discarded clothes.

He hovered above me, his hands tracing the curves of my breasts. "You really are exquisite," he breathed as he lowered his head to my bra and pulled at it with his teeth, his hand moving to my back and releasing the clasp. His hot breath against my nipple drove me crazy as I arched against him, the only thing separating us were my panties and his Armani underwear.

His hands moved across my hipbones and settled, pushing

against my mound, his thumb moving in small circles across my opening.

"Take them off," I begged as my nails grazed up and down his arms, desperate to feel skin on skin contact.

He inhaled sharply as I palmed him, having managed to push his underwear down enough to expose his hard, throbbing cock.

"Alexia." He moaned, lifting himself off me so he could kick off his Armani's before hooking his fingers into the waistband of my panties and sliding them off in one fluid movement, replacing them with his mouth.

"Ah!" I cried out as his tongue penetrated me without warning. His eyes were fierce as his thumb pressing against my clitoris while he continued to tongue me. Sensations flooded me as he made contact with my most sensitive skin, but it wasn't enough. I wanted to *touch* him, *taste* him and *feel* him in me.

"I want to suck you." I demanded as my hands fisted his hair. "Give me your cock." The words left my mouth in a rush and I didn't care how crude I sounded. Blushing wallflower I was not, and if Riccardo hadn't worked that out yet he was sure to be getting the memo soon.

"Alexia, can I at least finish what I started?" He gently lapped at my inner thigh, teasing the edges of my core.

"You can finish while your cock is in my mouth." I pulled his hair and yanked his head back.

"Demanding." He smirked as he gazed at me from in between my legs. "I've never been with a woman who was so assertive in bed."

"I'm not like most girls and if I'm having sex then I am sure as hell participating. Is that going to be a problem?" Probably a conversation we should have had *before* we got naked but better late than never. I was willing to do virtually anything sexually, but lying there and being fucked while I idly moaned was *not* on that list.

"Not a problem. Just requires a little adjustment." He shuffled up the bed so he was lying beside me, leaning toward me and nibbling at my shoulder. "And the thought of my cock in your mouth while I lick you makes me so hard it hurts."

"Good." I smiled as I climbed on top of him, twisting my body so he would have easy access to lick me while I could blow him. He stilled as I wrapped my lips around his girth, my hands pumped, slowly moving from the base to the tip as I moved my mouth up and down.

"Alexia." He groaned as he buried his face in between my legs, his fingers teasing me while his tongue was unrelenting.

"Aghh," I hummed as I pushed him as far down my throat as I could, my hands continuing to stroke him before pulling out his cock and swirling my tongue around the tip. Not everyone liked giving blowjobs but I freaking loved it and doing it while a guy went down on you was probably the ultimate. It felt so good I could barely see straight.

I felt Riccardo push a finger inside of me, stretching me before sliding in a second. Wetness dripped down my thigh as he continued to flick his tongue across my clit and every cell in my body felt like it was on fire.

"Alexia," Riccardo kissed the apex of my thigh. "I'm not sure how much longer I can hold out. Your mouth... it's so good."

"Don't stop." I begged, "Please don't stop." I was close, I could feel it and knowing he was holding back just about made me come right then.

He placed his mouth on my core again as I continued to lick and suck him, my body shook in anticipation as I felt myself tighten around his fingers.

"Alexia." My name sounded like a primal growl, ripping at his throat.

"YES." I panted as my body convulsed, pleasure rolling through me.

"Yes," Riccardo moaned as he finally let himself go and shot his load deep into my throat. I swallowed hard while I milked him with my hand, feeling his body jerk with the remnants of his orgasm.

He was still semi hard when I slid him from my mouth and rolled off of his body, twisting myself around so I was lying beside him.

"Are you always so aggressive?" Riccardo pulled my body closer to him.

"Generally. I can play it sweet when I want to, but right now I didn't want to." I smirked as I trailed my finger across his tanned pecs.

Riccardo laughed, "Despite your self-assurance you are still most definitely sweet." He dipped his head and kissed my shoulder. "I've tasted you myself."

4

The Great Escape

RICCARDO, it seemed, wasn't happy with just one taste and so when a few minutes later I climbed on top of him he was only too willing to show me how talented he was with other parts of his body.

"Alexia," Riccardo hissed in my ear as his hands guided my hips down while he rocked against me, filling me with each thrust. "Let go," he demanded as he felt me tighten around his shaft, I was so close.

I closed my eyes and I arched my back, giving him deeper access. I was torn between wanting this feeling to last forever and allowing myself to finish. I teetered on the edge, desperately trying to prolong it.

"Argh!" I cried out as I felt myself unable to hold on any longer. My body thrashed above him as he continued to move, throwing my nerve endings into a tailspin.

"That's it. Yes. Yes." He panted as I felt him explode inside of me, the thin latex sheath of the condom the only barrier between us.

I shook uncontrollably, the muscle fatigue setting in as I collapsed on top of him. I needed to get into shape. While walking around town had kept me toned, I was going to have to lift my game and actually exercise if I wanted to continue to have sex like that.

Riccardo was fit. Not just fit, but conditioned. Having rowed crew while at Harvard (something he divulged when I asked about the crossed oar tattoo that adorned his hip) and having a healthy gym obsession, he was barely breaking a sweat while he put me through my paces. In order to improve my fitness level, I was going to need either a structured régime or to keep screwing Riccardo, neither of which was really an option.

"You tired, *bella*?" His chest shook with laughter as I lay across it, utterly spent. I'd never had problems keeping up with a man before, the sleepiness that had overcome me was a new and unwelcome sensation.

As much as I wanted to close my eyes and bask in the afterglow, I couldn't go to sleep. That wasn't part of the plan. No, it was sex and then leave. No strings and usually no call back, though I sometimes relented and bent that rule if the participant proved worthy of a repeat performance. In most cases though, it was just easy to move on and in a city that teemed with tourists, this was not a difficult task.

"I just need a minute." I breathed heavily against his toned skin. Seriously, I was going to have to start running the Spanish Steps in the evenings. I had never been this puffed.

"Sleep, Alexia. We have the room until the morning and we both have probably consumed too much wine to drive. In the morning we can have breakfast and I will walk you to your car." He brushed the hair away from my face and slid me gently onto my side.

"Ok," I mumbled thinking I could get at least an hour or two and then slip out unnoticed before he woke up. Actually, that probably would work out better with no awkward "good-bye, thanks but I'm probably not going to call you" conversation. Besides, my legs were pretty much useless. I didn't think I could move, let alone walk. I was definitely going to have to start working out.

He shifted, lifting himself off of the bed and walked to the bathroom, treating me to the most amazing view of his taut and quite spectacular ass. I didn't care if he caught me staring, he was deserving of my attention. I wonder how many squats he did? I could definitely help him with pelvic thrusts should he need assistance. I couldn't help but smile at the thought.

I heard the toilet flush and then the water running signalled that he would soon be back. Unable to help myself, my eyes stayed focused on the door wanting to get a glimpse of his cock which in the frenzy to get into me (either my mouth or other parts of me), I hadn't been given the opportunity to appreciate.

He smirked as he walked back into the room, comfortable being completely naked and why wouldn't you when you looked like that? He was, in every sense of the word, breathtaking. Beautiful even. His body was flawless, his toned skin unmarked except for a tattoo on either hip (the crossed oars on one and some kind of eight-pointed star on the other) and his *package* - nothing short of impressive. His clothes that lay strewn across the floor were guilty of a most horrendous crime. Covering *that* up was unforgiveable.

"You like what you see?" He slid back into bed, stretching his arms behind his head so that his muscles flexed in the most delicious way.

"Yes, I do." I smiled, knowing that it would be probably be the last time I looked at it. He had certainly been the most interesting lay I'd had in a while and without a doubt the most energetic.

I closed my eyes and pretended to sleep. As much as I wanted to, I couldn't stay the night. The morning walk of shame always bought complications I didn't need. It was better this way, despite me wanting to see him again, wanting to feel him inside me one more time. Bad move, the sex had obviously messed with my mind. I needed to get out of here before I started having other stupid thoughts like snuggling.

I waited until his breathing slowed and his body relaxed. I turned slowly and watched the steady rise and fall of his chest. He was asleep. I carefully scooted to the edge of the bed, watching him for any movements but he didn't even stir. Satisfied, I was home free I slowly planted my feet on the floor and moved off of the mattress. Nothing. His breathing had remained unchanged, not even a muscle had twitched. He was out for the count and it was time for me to make for the door.

I quickly and quietly moved around the room gathering my clothes that had been randomly flung across the floor. I pulled on my panties, followed by my bra as I continued my surveillance of Riccardo. Still nothing, perfect. I grabbed my dress and pulled it over my head, twisting my arms around toward my back comically as I zipped myself up while the man I had fucked an hour ago lay blissfully unaware in front of me.

I tiptoed around the room and tried to locate the shoes I had carelessly tossed along with my clutch. Unable to keep watching him, I strained to hear for any changes to his breathing but thankfully there was nothing.

I finally found the offending black pumps under the bedspread Riccardo had so violently tossed on the floor. Good move on his part, I watch enough CSI to know there was an obscene amount DNA on those things without adding my contribution.

I spied my clutch on a chair near the door. I thanked my fore-thinking self for placing it somewhere easy to find, unlike the lust filled Lexi who tossed her shit around the room making present Lexi eat up valuable evacuation time.

With my shoes in hand, I tiptoed toward the door with the knowledge I was no more than twenty steps from being home free. I grabbed my clutch and pulled out some cash. I tossed some notes onto the chair, hoping it would at least cover half of the room cost. I knew he could afford it and didn't need my shitty Euro but it was a principle thing for me and my pride was pretty much everything these days. I had just placed my free hand (not the one balancing my shoes and my bag) on the door handle when I turned, glancing over my shoulder to take one final look.

"Not even going to say goodbye?" Riccardo was sitting up in bed, apparently as stealth-like as I was in his movements.

"Ummm." I paused, wondering if I should come clean or play it off like I was stepping out for some air. Hell, why even bother? Who cared what he thought? "I just thought it'd be easier." I turned around and faced him. There would be no quick-getaway apparently.

"You're leaving money? I've never been paid for sex before." He folded his arms across his chest, an amused look on his face.

"I'm not paying you for sex. It was to help cover the cost of the room." I tried to clarify wondering whether he was going to be flying off the handle any time soon. I should just leave. It's not like he would chase me naked down the hallway.

"You don't think I could cover it?" He smirked as his eyebrow rose. Of course he could afford the room, he could probably buy this hotel. The whole situation seemed to amuse him; he didn't even seem annoyed I was about to attempt a hit-and-run.

"Whether you could or couldn't afford the room is not the issue. I used the room with you and therefore I wanted to contribute." It sounded so much cooler in my head. I wanted to contribute? Probably could have thought of something more intelligent to say or just gotten the fuck out instead of hesitating.

"I have to say I'm a little surprised. I would have thought the kind of person who has sex and then disappears would be *taking* money out of my wallet not trying to *put it in*." He unfolded his arms, allowing one to rub the base of his chin. His eyes gleamed with mischief.

What? He had thought I was going to rummage through his wallet? The crack I had made at lunch about being a thief was just that, a joke. I didn't take advantage of men... well not in *that* way.

"I'm not a con-artist or a grifter. I didn't sleep with you so I could steal your shit. I had sex with you because I wanted to have sex with you."

"And then leave when you were done." He gestured to the door. His voice was devoid of the anger I had heard from other men in this situation.

"Oh come on Riccardo. Honestly, what did you think was going to happen here? A relationship? You just slept with a woman you met ten hours ago. You must have known what this was. We both got off, what more is there?" I guess if we were laying our cards on the table we might as well lay them all out. It's not like there had been any indication from either of us that this was going to be anything more than a one night stand.

Riccardo laughed, leaning back against the headboard, not even attempting to hide his enjoyment of the situation. He was laughing! He was fucking laughing like it was all some kind of joke and he was thoroughly amused.

His toned steadied (when he was done laughing his ass off) as he engaged me with his gaze. "Oh you are marvellous, you know that? Simply marvellous. I knew there was something about you that was remarkable and it wasn't just that amazing little body of yours, which as you put it *got me off*."

"Huh? You're not angry?" I was still not grasping what was going on here. In the past, I had been subjected to the gamut of responses, everything from thanking me for my time to the angry, almost stalking that followed days later demanding an explanation. Who said that bullshit was reserved solely for teenage girls? Jilted men apparently could pull drama too if given a chance which is why I chose to eject earlier rather than later.

"Why would I be angry? I've never been paid for sex before. Tell me, how much were those orgasms worth?" He slid off the bed (unperturbed by the fact he was naked) and walked over to the chair, picking up the crumpled notes. He raised an eyebrow, before pouting comically. "45 Euro? Disappointing."

"Well I didn't want to say anything but I have had better." I couldn't help but giggle at the situation.

"I demand the opportunity for regaining my honour." He tossed the notes back onto the chair and stalked closer to me.

"Riccardo, let's not ruin it. Last night was fun. If you are smart you should let me just walk out." His close proximity in his delightfully nude state made all humour evaporate. Yeah, not so easy to laugh when you have a hot Demi-God standing toe to toe with you. I fought valiantly against my inner desire not to lower my eyes to his cock though I was positive it deserved another look. Instead I kept my eyes raised; someone needed to give me a medal or something.

"Why?" He moved closer, his face inches from mine, taking my shoes from my hand and placing them on the chair.

"Why what?" I shrugged, confused as to which part of my statement he was questioning. I guess despite me telling Riccardo this was not a good idea, I was staying a little longer.

He removed the clutch from my hand and gave it the opportunity to join my shoes. Considerate of him, they really did enjoy being together. "Why should I let you walk out? Alexia, you know who I am and yet you didn't try and steal from me or use me. That is quite a unique experience for me, especially here in Roma." He ran his finger along my jaw, tilting my head to meet his eyes.

"Well technically I did use you, for your body at least." I smirked wondering if it was too soon to *use* him again. He seemed open to the idea and let's face it, him being completely cool with me was really turning me on.

"You didn't use me. I was fully aware of what your intentions were." He moved his mouth closer so it hovered over mine.

"So you knew we'd end up here? So sure of yourself?" I kept my eyes glued to his lips knowing what would happen if he kissed me.

"Alexia, you are a beautiful woman. I wanted you as much as you wanted me but no, I was not sure." He moved his mouth to my neck and trailed kisses up to the base of my ear.

"So now what? Did you want have sex again?" I could hear my voice waver. Damn it Lexi! Get your shit together. I was disappointed my resolve had started to wane, I could see it walking out the door like I should have done five minutes ago.

"I'm positive you wouldn't have enough Euro in your purse to cover the next orgasm." He whispered into my ear, pretty much guaranteeing that my panties were going to be soaked by the end of this conversation.

"Don't be so sure. I might be a secret heiress, I could be

loaded for all you know." I offered with as much conviction as I could muster. I had no illusions I was fooling anyone.

Riccardo pulled me away from the door, guiding me toward the bed. I offered no resistance. "That would be very disappointing. I like you. You are so refreshing and I don't sleep with heiresses."

"Why? From what I have gathered they more your kind, aren't they?" I would have thought that he would have been mainlining rich girls with trust funds. Granted they were probably high maintenance and I don't think the quaint little restaurant with the "best pizza in Rome" would fly as a date, nor the alleyway make-out session.

He pulled on his pants, commando, and displayed the first inkling of frustration. "They are predictable and they bore me. My path was chosen from before I took my first step and in time I will be expected to marry someone who is suitable. It's quite a small pool." He sat on the edge of the bed and raked his hands through his mess of dark brown waves.

"Such a hardship. Do you want me to hand you a Kleenex?" I slurred sarcastically. Was he expecting sympathy? Boo-fucking-hoo. Saddled with money and family expectations, the horror. I saw no one holding a gun to his head.

"Wow, I see once you've achieved your objective you don't hold back. I didn't think I could be any more attracted to you." Ricardo laughed, once again surprising me by not being offended by my big-ass mouth. He must be some kind of freak. He was getting some of my best material and nothing was rattling him.

"I'm sure it will pass." I deadpanned standing in front of him.

"It doesn't have to. In fact, I think this would work out very nicely for me." His mouth curled as I could see the cogs in his brain ticking over. He was devising some kind of plan but doing little to clue me in.

"What are you talking about?"

"You. Me. Us. Yes, I think we should definitely continue." He moved his two fingers between us to illustrate what he was talking about. Just as well I might add, because I wasn't fully comprehending his proposition. Trust the hot guy I just fucked to be insane. Serves me right, I really should screen better.

An involuntary laugh escaped my lips, I was unable to suppress my amusement. Insanity or not, it was time to set him straight. "I love how you think you have any choice in this matter but there is no us. It was a one-time deal. There will be no continuing."

"If we both suit each other's needs, I can't see the problem. And Alexia, I always have a choice." Riccardo argued his voice a mix of arrogance and confidence. He didn't flinch or laugh - he was serious, further confirming my earlier assessment of insanity.

"I don't do relationships." I hissed, slightly annoyed we were still having this conversation. I would have been happy with more sex but now he was talking about something more. I didn't do *more*.

"Such an overused word." He cringed, giving me a glimmer of hope that he wasn't going to ask me to be his girlfriend.

"So what's in this for you?" I sat beside him, my interest piqued about what exactly he was going to get out of it. It's not like he had to be hard up for choices. Why me?

"As I said, my life's path has been predetermined. I'm not yet ready to be shackled however I would very much like to be in your company." He smiled. I guess he wasn't insane after all, just after convenient sex. I had to admit, I was tempted. It would solve my earlier conundrum about how I was going to improve my fitness.

"In what capacity? Do we organise appointments for sex? Have a regular day? I'm not really interested in being anyone's play thing." If I was doing this, it was still going to be on my terms.

"You are not a whore Alexia and I will not treat you like one. Yes I want to continue to have sex with you but I require a little more." There was that word, more. He held his hand up to silence my simmering rebuttal. "Not in the way you are think-ing. I want us to be friends Alexia, I want to spend time with you."

"I'm not sure your family are going to be down with your choice of associations. They may excuse your discreet indiscre-tions but being friendly with me is something I'm sure they won't overlook." I was not ashamed of who I was but I knew there were differences between us and that assumptions would be made. I was a lot of things, a gold-digger was not one of them.

"Good. Let them," he smirked, the lack of surprise evident on his face.

"Wait! You *want* to piss them off? You want for them to disapprove." Like finding the missing puzzle piece it all came together. He was rebelling. He wanted to dance on the shadier side of the street while giving his parents the big F U and dating me would certainly provide that opportunity. I probably should have been angry but strangely, I was impressed. There was no reason why it couldn't work. No danger of us ending up together long term, he'd made that clear. As for me, I too was bored with the same old, same old - maybe it would be fun.

"Alexia, up until this point I have done everything by my father's grand scheme. He won't control who I date." He confirmed.

"So you want to use me to prove a point?" I laughed. His parents would pitch a fit when they found out, their youngest son who had recently graduated from Harvard Business School was dating a waitress. A foreign waitress.

"I have a lot of uses for you, and you for me no doubt. You've already proven how smart you are, I have a lot to offer you as well." He tilted his face, a genuine smile lighting up his features.

"Like what? I don't need anything you have." I shrugged. What could he possibly offer me? There is no way I'd take cash. I had a place to stay and a job, so what else was there?

"Alexia, I don't know you. We just met, but in the few hours I have spent with you I can tell it's been a while since you have had real passion in your life. Maybe you have never had it. Stop playing with boys. Play with me instead." Riccardo's eyes simmered with promise. Yeah he had my number, there *was* something else. Something he could offer me.

"I do my own thing. I don't like rules and I don't need a keeper." I was happy to *play* girlfriend but if he started invoking privileges that he hadn't earned, I'd be walking no matter how good the sex was.

"You will get none of that from me. I'm not looking for a pet. Just a companion who will not bore me to tears, with the added benefit of sex."

"So we do this publically?" I clarified, wanting to know how far he wanted to take this ruse.

"The sex? Are you an exhibitionist?" His eyebrows rose in question. I couldn't tell if he was joking or hopeful.

I bumped his shoulder. Ass! "No, I mean are we going to *date* publically?"

"Yes." He answered with no hesitation.

"I won't be controlled." I gave him a sideways glance, giving him one more chance for an out.

"I've already had sex with you Alexia, I am aware you like

to be in control. I never thought I would enjoy that, but now that I have had a taste..." He paused as he moved his hand up my thigh. "I want to taste it again."

"I'm warning you. I'm going to be trouble for you."

"I was counting on it."

5

Morning Disturbances

"YOU DID IT, DIDN'T YOU?" I was awoken by Stefania's pillow bouncing off the top of my head.

"Stefania." I squinted not ready for my eyes to deal with the sunlight that was rudely streaming into the room. "It's early. Let me sleep." I groaned into my pillow.

"Tell me Lexi! You walked in here early this morning. I heard you. You nailed him didn't you?" She was unrelenting as she pummelled me again with her pillow. This was getting old, real quick.

I sat up in bed and grabbed the pillow from her hands before she had a chance to hit me a third time. "I think the word you are looking for is *screwed* him Stefania, and yes I did. What does it matter?"

"Lexi, he will burn you. He is not one of us. Stay away from him." Her head bounced from side to side in warning.

"Stefania, aren't you taking it a little too far?" I scrubbed my face with my hands. "Besides weren't you out with Josh last night? How is that any different?"

"It's different." Stefania pouted dramatically. "And," her voice rose an octave, "I didn't sleep with him!"

"Did you blow him?"

"Lexi! A lady never tells." She squealed in mock horror. All the verification I required was written on her face.

"Stefania, you are adorable and predictable." I shook my head as I struggled to contain my smile. "So are we still having this conversation or can I go back to sleep?"

"Ok so the damage is done. You had a Cassius. Paint it up to an experience and move on. We find you someone else." She sighed, wrongly assuming that I was done with him.

"I'm seeing him again." I figured it was easier to just get it over with considering I wasn't going to be hearing the end of it any time soon. Besides, if Riccardo and I were going to keep up appearances she would find out soon enough.

"Lexi!" Stefania gasped in shock.

"Stefania!" I parodied. "He isn't like them. I'm telling you he's different and we're going to be seeing each other so you're just going to have to get over your hang ups." It felt weird defending our pseudo-relationship but I didn't want to have to hear how horrible he was just because his family had a reputation. Besides, we were probably going to be getting enough shit from his *family*, I didn't need to get it here as well.

"You're going to date him? Lexi, you don't date anyone." Stefania's mouth fell open and her eyes bulged. In the three months that I had spent with her she'd never seen me date anyone. Not more than twice anyway.

"Well maybe it's time I did. He's a nice guy Stefania. I want to get to know him. This merry-go-round I'm on is a little stale. It will be good to be with someone regular for a while." I shrugged.

Maybe this might actually turn out to be a good thing, being with one guy. Lots of people did it and we had an understanding so we didn't have to worry about messy emotions getting in the way.

"Did he drug you?" She slapped her hand to my forehead. "Are you sick? He must have put something in your drink, because you have lost the theme."

"I haven't lost the *plot* and I am not sick." I pulled her hand away from my face.

"How big is it then?" She whispered despite no one other than us being around to hear her.

"Huh?"

"His dick must be HUGE if you are giving up other lovers." She gave up any pretense of being discreet and threw out her hands in her playful display.

"So what happened to a lady doesn't tell? I'm not discussing his penis size with you. All I will say is that he made me happy, *repeatedly* and I'm not looking to sleep with anyone else."

"HUUUUUUUGGGGGGEEEE" She sang, elongating the word for effect.

"No comment." I laughed, not willing to give the topic any more airtime.

"It's fine, all is revealed by your silence." Stefania smirked in satisfaction. She was right he was more than adequate (ok pretty freaking big), but she wouldn't be hearing that from me.

"Ok. I'm going back to sleep then. Your car keys are on the bureau." I shuffled back down into bed and laid my head on the pillow. I shut my eyes tightly trying to ignore Stefania sitting beside me on the bed, showing no signs of moving.

"I can feel you watching me and it's kind of creepy."

"I want to tell you about Josh." She bounced up and down on the bed like a three year old.

"I thought we weren't talking about it." I mumbled, unwilling to open my eyes.

"Come on Lexi. I need to tell you or I will pop." Stefania whined, shaking my arm.

"Fine, talk, but I'm keeping my eyes shut." I conceded, knowing I was fighting a losing battle against the sleep I was chasing.

Stefania babbled in her excited voice, giving me a detailed report from the moment he picked her up at the trattoria until the moment he dropped her back at our apartment. Apparently any hesitation she may have had about revealing our place of residence had been alleviated throughout the evening. I imagined that was sometime between the main course where he told her he had a business degree from Harvard (something I already knew) and the blowjob she gave him in the car where he told her she had the most impressive tits he'd ever seen, (granted they were pretty amazing).

I "A-ah-ed" and "Hmm-ed" a few times to prove I was listening but my eyes remained shut and at some point I must have drifted off to sleep because the next thing I heard was a loud banging coming from the front door.

"I'm coming." I called out as I groggily stumbled out of bed.

The apartment was empty, with Stefania's excited chatter noticeably absent. I pulled on a pair of shorts, not wanting to treat my unannounced visitor to a surprise view of me in a pair of panties and a tank top (I didn't do pajamas) and ambled to the front door.

"I'm coming." I called out again for no particular reason, as I yanked on the doorknob and pulled it open.

"Good Morning." Josh smiled in the doorway, his eyes floating down toward my chest, the tank top doing little to disguise that I was bra-less.

"Oh. Hey." I yawned, too tired to care that I probably

looked like shit. "Stefania isn't here, she is probably at work. She had the early shift today."

"Oh Shoot. I was hoping to catch her. We had a really good time last night and Ric mentioned you guys had hit it off too." He gave me a clichéd quick wink.

"Yeah she said you guys had fun." I leaned up against the doorframe, deliberately ignoring the last part of his sentence. Riccardo didn't seem like the type of guy to gossip so I assumed any information Josh had would be purely speculation.

"So what do you ladies have planned for this evening?" Josh smiled, seemingly content to stand out in the hallway.

"I don't have Stefania's social calendar I'm sorry. You can probably stop by work and check with her though, I'm sure she'd be happy to see you." I tried to stifle another yawn unsuccessfully.

Stefania loved attention and her ample assets meant there was no shortage of admirers. She was also a helpless romantic, which meant she fell in love frequently. Of course soon enough she'd just as easily fall out of love or someone else would spark her interest and then she would have to break the poor sucker's heart. Some would even try to win her back with extravagant gifts and over-the-top declarations of devotion (can you say stalker?) and while it would send most women running as fast as they could in the opposite direction, Stefania loved it. Call it a character flaw or a need for attention, the harder they tried, the more impressed she seemed. So while I thought an unannounced visit from Harvard Josh was kind of creepy, Stefania would eat it up with a spoon.

"I can do that, but I was hoping you might join us as well. Go out as a group. Maybe hit a club?"

"As in, the three of us?" Goddamn Stefania and her big ass mouth! She had probably told this dude about her not-so-secret desire to bed me and he was probably thinking Christmas had come early this year. It was too fucking early in the day to be considering a threesome.

"No, silly. I was going to invite Riccardo as well." Josh grinned, thankfully not following my train of thought. "Tom and Shawn have some weird card game they are trying to master and I can't make heads or tails of it. Looks nothing like the decks we have back home." He shrugged before continuing, "Anyway, both of them are pretty serious poker players so a new card game has them fascinated, they won't be leaving the apartment tonight. Thought the two of you lovely ladies could join us out on the town. It's kind of getting old, hanging with a bunch of dudes."

"You think this up on your own or was it a team decision?" I arched my brow sceptically. Riccardo didn't seem like the type of guy who would send someone else to do his bidding so I had to assume Josh was bootlegging this play.

"Nah, it's just me. Back in the States I couldn't drag Riccardo away from the clubs till mornin' but here he is totally avoiding the scene. Girls end up buzzing around him like bar flies so I guess that's why he tends to give it a wide berth. However, I'm sure your inclusion to the outing would guarantee Riccardo's participation. See, I'm a card player too and I know how to stack a deck."

"He could say no." I argued, not sure Riccardo would appreciate plans being made without his consultation.

"He won't." Josh smirked smugly.

"I could say no."

"I'm betting *you* won't." His smiled widened.

"I'm working till 9 tonight and I'll need to change." I rubbed my neck, mentally calculating whether or not I actually wanted to do this.

"So we'll go when you're ready. No big deal. We can either pick you up from work or here, whatever you like. So we good?"

59

"You still need to get Riccardo to agree."

"Leave Ric to me. You just give me the ok and I'll make it happen."

"Sure." I conceded, not really having any solid plans for the night. "But you're buying drinks. Club-priced spirits are criminal and I refuse to blow my rent money on expensive vodka, lime and sodas. Oh, and leave the fancy watch at home. The clubs are filled with pickpockets and lowlifes so unless you want to be filling out an insurance claim tomorrow, don't attract attention to yourself."

"Done. Drinks are on me and I'll do my best to be inconspicuous."

"You're American, you don't have the capacity to be inconspicuous. Just dial down the bling and try not to be too loud." I mused sarcastically.

Josh let out a large boisterous laugh (further proving my point on the loud issue). "Just tell me where you want us to meet you and I'll work on keeping it on the down low."

"Meet me at work. I'll change there." It was easier just to bring clothes to work than to back-track home to my apartment.

"Perfect! I'll go square everything away with Stefania and Ric and we'll meet you out the front at 9. And Lexi, thanks." Josh reached out and awkwardly rubbed my arm.

"Don't thank me yet, you haven't seen how many vodka, lime and sodas you're up for." My lips twitched with the knowledge that most men underestimated my drinking capacity.

"I'm pretty sure I can handle it." I had no doubt that his cocky smile was backed up by a sizeable bank account.

"Well...this has been great. We should definitely do impromptu hall conversations more often but if we're done here, I might try and get some sleep. Surprisingly, it has been hard to come by this morning."

"Sure, sure. I'll leave you to it." Josh backed away from the door with a friendly wave.

"Later." I closed the door, hoping that was the last of the morning interruptions.

I didn't even bother heading to my bed, my earlier pursuit abandoned. Instead I padded over to the couch and let the cushions envelop my body.

Another date with Riccardo. I hadn't planned on seeing him so soon but I'll admit that the thought of another night with him thrilled me. Maybe it was because he was deemed unsuitable or maybe it was because he had an impressive cock and he knew how to use it. Ha! I should probably go start running steps in preparation. Either way, this illicit affair excited me and I liked that emotion. Excitement was something I could work with, it sure as hell was more valuable than love and about a hundred times more constructive.

6

Night-time Rush

"WHAT HAPPENED TO DIALLING IT DOWN?" I frowned as Riccardo held open the door of the very conspicuous black limo parked in front of the trattoria.

"This was Josh's solution so no one had to drive tonight." Riccardo's eyes followed the lines of my body as he slithered into the car. "You look stunning Alexia."

"Thank you." I smiled in appreciation, noticing it was the first time I'd seen him not wearing a suit. Instead he was dressed in black jeans, heavy boots and a black fitted t-shirt, his version of slumming it no doubt.

"We'll get the car to drop us off. I'll keep the fanfare to a minimum." Josh winked as Riccardo took his seat beside me.

"Whatever. It's your cash." I rolled my eyes, pretending to be bored.

"I think the car is sexy." Stefania lilted as she snuggled up closer to Josh. "Lexi, don't be such a bee kill."

"It's *buzz* kill." I corrected as Riccardo gently placed his hand on my bare thigh. I had opted for one of the few designer dresses I owned. Purchased last year in an end of season sale, the red crepe material clung to my body like it had been made specifically for me. Simple in its design, the plunging neckline of the mini dress vetoed any idea of it being boring. It was my first Versace and it made me feel like a million bucks.

Stefania stuck out her tongue, her usual response when she refused to acknowledge her mistakes. It was hard to believe she was actually three months older than me.

Stefania and Josh's conversation dominated the ride to the club. The two seemed to have an endless amount of words to sprout between them, with Riccardo occasionally breaking up the linguistic monopoly. I was happy to relax in the soft leather seats, having no interest in injecting my thoughts on any of their topics of conversation, but I was glad that Stefania had warmed to Riccardo - or at the very least, gave the appearance that her stance on him being the Devil's seed had softened.

The limo slowed to a stop at the front of one of Rome's premier clubs, *Fuoco*. The bass of the music spilled out onto the street as we climbed out of the car and ambled to the front door. There was a queue, but the line moved efficiently with several bouncers weeding out candidates who would not be entering the establishment no matter how long they stood outside. It was probably a little heavy-handed but Italians had their own way of doing things. Arguing the merit in the way these things were done would not get you in any faster. In fact, it would probably get your ass thrown out. So it was best to keep your mouth shut, smile and lubricate the hands of WWF wannabes who controlled the traffic flow. Regardless of its injustice, the system was not changing.

Once we had satisfied the requirements at the door and were allowed entry, we were treated to the display of frenzied bodies on the dance floor convulsing to amplified Eurotrash.

The strobe lights washed over the sea of heads and raised arms, the air thick with sweat and sex. European clubs were not for spectating, the unrestrained energy demanded participation - something the patrons had no problem providing as they indulged in various incarnations of excess.

"Dance with me!" Stefania squealed as she pulled Josh through the horde of hypnotized humans. They too became lost in the menagerie within minutes.

"Alexia," Riccardo pulled me to his body, his hands sliding down to my ass. "While I love that dress on you, I think I will enjoy it more when I am peeling it from your body later tonight."

"You could probably peel it from my body right now, I don't think anyone here would notice." I half-laughed into his ear.

"You *are* an exhibitionist." His hand tightened around my ass, an amused grin flirting on his lips.

"I can be. I'm very versatile."

"Something I'm looking forward to exploring." Riccardo guided us away from the dance floor, avoiding the fevered bodies gyrating under the flickering lights.

We found a dark corner where we were able to speak without shouting, the mismatched beat with no lyrics was only slightly less obnoxious when not blaring.

Riccardo pulled me close, my body melding into his as we danced privately, without a need for a sanctioned area. His arms wrapped tightly around my waist as I moved against him. A bead of sweat trickled down my neck. His eyes darkened as he bowed his head and licked it, tasting me.

"You're delicious." He growled in my ear.

"I like your tongue on me." I bit my lip as I ran my hands through his hair. While we weren't on the dance floor, we certainly weren't alone either. Partygoers milled around us, largely uninterested in our actions. No doubt they were sharing *our* brilliant idea to use the periphery of the club for a more private sort of enthusiastic physical display.

"I would have preferred to take you home and tongue you in private." Riccardo nipped at my shoulder, the bulge I felt against my hip hinting that he would be using more than just his tongue.

"Hey, don't blame me. It was *your* friend who orchestrated this. I was home minding my own business when he practically begged for me to come." I playfully swatted at his chest. I'd have preferred the private show as well.

"He has been trying to get me to this place for days," Riccardo rolled his eyes before settling into a grin. "And he seems quite taken with your friend."

"Just to let you know, Stefania will probably break his heart. I adore her but she falls in and out of love so frequently I can't keep up." I felt the need to qualify, and I hoped Josh's plane ticket back to the US of A was booked before Stefania's infatuation expired.

"He is a big boy. I'm sure he can handle it."

While Riccardo seemed unconcerned for his friend's possible heartache, my interest was piqued about why he had put the hex on local clubs. Josh had mentioned that while Riccardo had no issue with the nightlife in Boston, he was a reluctant participant in his hometown. I wasn't chalking it up to being God-fearing, a man who fucked like that wasn't usually afraid of hell.

"So why have you been avoiding clubs? It can't be the immorality, you didn't seem to have a problem with question-able decisions yesterday."

"Is that how you see yourself? A questionable decision?" He tilted his head, perhaps hoping his side step of the question went unnoticed.

"We weren't talking about me, we were talking about you.

Stop avoiding." Curiosity superseded politeness as my mouth once again opened of its own volition. It really was a talent.

"Because in Roma, everyone knows who I am and who my family is. They are not interested in *Riccardo*, they are interested because I am a *Cassius*. I don't have the patience for it."

He had given me the poor-rich guy routine yesterday and honestly, I had taken it with a grain of salt but perhaps his life was actually challenged by his genealogy. A man that looked like that should be enjoying a serious amount of pussy, not avoiding situations that foster the opportunity.

"I think you are underselling yourself. I'm sure there are lot of women who just want to sleep with you because you look like a sex God."

"You think I look like a sex God? Did you come to this conclusion before or after I made you come?"

He seemed genuinely amused by the classification. Surely he wasn't surprised. He went to college in Boston, those girls wouldn't have known or cared who his daddy was. If Josh was half as good a friend as he claimed to be, he would have seen to it that Riccardo had been offered the FULL college experience.

"Oh before! Which is the reason I allowed you the opportunity to make me come." It was not a lie, I had sized him up and deemed him worthy even before Stefania had freaked out at the bar, the added element of danger had just made it more appealing.

"So the only reason you went to that hotel with me last night was because of my face?" His didn't even try to suppress his grin.

"The body too, I liked the whole package. The money and the reputation, I can't say it really impresses me, sorry." I pretended to be bored.

"Don't be sorry, I love that you aren't impressed." Riccardo kissed my neck, his hands getting busy on my ass. Really, why were we still here and not back at my place getting horizontal?

"So we're good, me using you for sex then? I hope so. I've got a purse full of Euro for the orgasms you promised."

"I told you last night Alexia, you couldn't afford me. Lucky for you, I'm happy for the mutual exchange of exploitation." He pushed me against his erection. There was a lot to be said for the barter system.

"Riccardo." A voice called out through the noise-filled fog, disrupting our moment. The tone demanded attention. "Riccardo."

We turned to the direction of the voice, as a tall, athletic and rather good-looking figure emerged from the crowd.

"Hey. *Ho pensato che eri tu. Cosa fai qui? Chi è la ragazza?*" The owner of the voice ignored me, and if I hadn't been able to translate that he was asking Riccardo what he was doing here and who the girl was, I wouldn't have been sure my existence had even been acknowledged. He hadn't even bothered to make eye contact.

"Hey Enzo, this is Alexia." Riccardo deliberately responded in English. "Alexia, this is one of my brothers, Enzo." He kept his arm protectively around my waist.

His brother. While we had spent a little time talking about Riccardo's family, we had not delved into the particulars other than the huge expectations his last name carried. Riccardo's introduction of Enzo as "one of my brothers" logically indicated more than one. How many of them were there and did they all look like they could grace the page of a *Dolce and Gabbana* ad? Riccardo was freaking gorgeous, and while Enzo was not as breathtaking as his sibling, he was still blessed with similarly striking features. While it appeared that this brother was an asshole, he was a genetically blessed asshole nonetheless.

"Little brother has a new toy. American?" Enzo's smile was

anything but sincere. It unnerved me and put me on the defensive.

"Australian." I corrected, not bothering to offer anything else in greeting. He was officially pissing me off.

"Same thing," Enzo scoffed, apparently content to live in the ignorance that all English speaking foreigners were Americans. Dumbass.

"You have to excuse Enzo," Riccardo apologized, "His understanding of geography doesn't extend beyond second grade. This is why he works with his hands."

"Oah!" Enzo laughed before rattling off words I couldn't follow but guessed to be playful obscenities. "Little brother is trying to impress you. He must like you." Enzo seemingly warmed for the first time since the start of our interaction as he held out his hand. "Work with my hands? I'm a mechanical engineer, don't listen to this donkey."

"Pleased to meet you." I shook his hand but mentally added him to my *watch* list. You know, the list of people you wouldn't trust even if the Dalai Lama vouched for them? It wasn't his arrogance that had won him the listing, it was the cagey vibe he was rocking. I had no legitimate basis for not trusting him, except a gut feeling that I refused to ignore.

With his hand still firmly grasped around mine he pulled me forward. "He may like you, foreigner, but you aren't here to stay." He hissed in my ear before releasing me. Point proven, in the end I didn't have to wait too long to feel vindicated over my snap judgement.

"Enzo!" Riccardo pushed his brother hard across the shoulder as he demanded, "What did you say to her?" He was annoyed but more than that, he was angry.

"You are too sensitive! Mamma babied you too long." Enzo laughed, unperturbed by Riccardo's mounting irritation.

The two of them locked eyes in a mental showdown and if

I'd been smart I would have kept my mouth shut and kept out of it. After all, this had nothing to do with me; I had merely been the catalyst for whatever shit was being stirred. But you see my mouth and I had a problem, one that involved me being unable to control what came out of it, despite knowing the trouble it would cause. Well I guess everyone needed a hobby.

I recaptured Enzo's hand pulling his ear close to my mouth, "I'm not here to stay," I smirked as I continued, "I'm just here to fuck your baby brother till he can't see straight and I assure you, there is nothing *sensitive* about the way he puts his cock in me."

Enzo pulled away from me in disgust. "Your whore has a filthy mouth." He gave his brother a hard but knowing look. "I'll see you later."

"She isn't a whore! Don't you dare speak to her like that," Riccardo spat angrily but Enzo simply turned and evaporated into the crowd from whence he had appeared.

"What did you say to him?" Riccardo mused, "I've never seen him back down so quickly."

"I'm not intimidated by your brother and I thought he needed to know that." I wrapped my arms around his neck. Being called a whore, with or without a filthy mouth, was nothing new and it did not bother me. Besides, I'd dealt with the likes of Enzo before, the ones who had wrongly assumed they were better than me. If he thought he had rattled my cage he would be sadly mistaken, all he did was wake my beast and I was not yet sure how far Riccardo was willing to play this thing. If we were really planning on putting on a public display, there was no way I would be backing down. I didn't have the capacity to disengage - perhaps that was my character flaw? I felt like I needed to give him one last chance for an out. "You still want to do this? 'Cause I think I just made things worse for you."

Riccardo's broad smile widened as the anger receded from his eyes. He took my chin with his hand and seized my mouth.

His kisses were hungry and aggressive, unrelenting in their pursuit to own every inch of me. I guess that made two of us who weren't backing down.

"After witnessing that, there isn't anything that could change my mind."

7

Legends and Vodka

IT TOOK me about five minutes to make Riccardo forget about his brother, until the simmering agitation had been transformed into a tension of a different kind. Another talent.

Josh and Stefania eventually emerged from the frenzied crowd, sweaty and dishevelled. While Stefania hadn't actually slept with him last night, she was clearly considering remedying that situation tonight. Considering the fact that her lips were permanently locked to his, I wasn't convinced they wouldn't be finding a bathroom and taking care of it *before* we left.

Riccardo managed to locate a booth (or rather he commandeered it from a bunch of star-struck eighteen year olds who probably would have given him their car had he asked) and we were able to sit down. Another one of the benefits of your family owning most of the town, I guess.

Josh honoured his word and kept the drinks flowing, paying a waitress a very generous tip to ensure that each time one of us hit the bottom of our glass, a fresh one would find its place. It was a very cool magic trick, one that saw me quickly lose track of how many vodka, lime and sodas I was consuming. My usual cautious façade slipped further as more magic glasses appeared. Riccardo lost his reserved pretense as well, openly laughing at Stefania who admitted to still believing he was the Devil.

"I can't help it!" She squeaked in-between giggles. "I was trying to be a good friend and I have heard the legends."

"The legends?" I struggled to breathe, the alcohol making everything abundantly more humorous. "You make him sound like a dragon." Stefania and her not-so-masterful command of the English language never failed to entertain, especially when they conjured up *Lord of the Rings* type analogies. I pulled firmly on Riccardo's shirt, "Do you breathe fire, Dragon?"

"Only when threatened, but mostly I try not to pee on the carpet." Riccardo teased, playfully kissing my neck.

"Oh, close up!" Stefania folded her arms across her chest indignantly.

"I think you mean *shut* up Sweetheart." Josh hugged her adoringly while trying to suppress his grin.

"My Nonna told me how Marcus Cassius poisoned the water wells, making those who didn't work for him sick. That was how he got so rich. The landowners died and Marcus bought all the land, the peasants begged to work on his farms so they could be spared the horrific death. No one dared defy him. And with the birth of each new generation, their influence grew. The Cassius men were so beautiful that virgins fell under their spell, bearing them numerous sons to continue their lega-cy." Stefania's face flushed with excitement before adding, pointing wildly at Riccardo. "You have three brothers. See. Four boys! Diavolo!"

I doubled over, unable to stop from laughing hysterically as Riccardo tried in vain to set Stefania straight. "I have plenty of girl cousins, those fables are made up. Marcus Cassius was a General for the Roman army. He was awarded land when he returned home having won numerous battles for the Empire. He didn't poison anyone and his third son, Julius, only had daughters."

"Ric, I don't think you are going to convince her." Josh howled pulling Stefania into a passionate embrace. "He's not the Devil darlin' just a sharp dresser with deep pockets."

I squeezed Riccardo's thigh as I continued to chuckle, "And I'm not a virgin so no need to worry about me falling under his spell."

"You didn't fall under Enzo's spell either. Perhaps you are immune to the Cassius charm." Riccardo knocked back his tumbler of amber liquid. Slumming would only go so far it seemed, and while Josh was drinking dirty martinis all night Riccardo sucked down twenty-year-old scotch, neat.

"That's because he is an asshole. Not even your magical last name is going to change that." I smiled, downing another drink. How many had that been? I had well and truly lost track.

"Enzo was here? I didn't see him." Josh bit into the tooth-pick-speared olive that had been swirling around in his drink.

"He didn't stay." Riccardo's brow rose as he smirked in my direction. Perhaps using some kind of boy-code to indicate I had been the reason for Enzo's hasty departure.

"Probably a good thing." Josh glanced at me, amused, before draining the rest of his martini. Yep, definitely boy-code.

"So there are four of you?" I interjected wanting to know more about Riccardo and his band of brothers. I wondered if the other two were as friendly as the one I had met.

"Yes, I am the youngest of four boys." A waitress set another tumbler of scotch in front of Riccardo before retrieving his empty glass. She gave him a nervous side-glance and a giggle when he nodded his head in thanks.

"And where does Enzo fit into the mix?" He didn't look much older than Riccardo but it was hard to tell.

"He is a year older than me. Then comes Nicholas, the second eldest but he hasn't been home in over two years. He is the one I'm closest to. He didn't want to be part of the family business so he is living in America, forging his own way. He owns restaurants and is doing very well for himself. I got to spend a lot of time with him while living there. Maybe someday we'll go visit. He'd love you." Riccardo spoke fondly of his middle brother but I could guarantee we wouldn't be visiting. I had little time for my own dysfunctional family, I didn't need to adopt someone else's.

"And Marcus is the oldest." Riccardo raised his palms in defence, "Yes, before you say anything, a lot of the men in the family are called Marcus, the name is passed down to the first born son."

"I told you." Stefania pumped her hands in the air, victorious like she'd won some grand prize. "I knew I was right."

Riccardo ignored Stefania's celebratory gloating. "He is married and my beautiful sister in law recently had a baby *girl*. He is the CEO of my father's corporation and very much my father's son."

"Is that supposed to mean that he too is an asshole?" No filter. I didn't even have the decency to be sorry, my blood alcohol level absolved me of any guilt.

"He's my brother Alexia and I love my family but we share very different philosophies." Translation - yes they are all assholes but I'm going to be diplomatic in the way I agree with you. That's ok, being right is still being right.

"Ok," I climbed into Riccardo's lap wanting his lips to stop talking about his family and get busy on me.

"You want me to take you home?" He read my cue and kissed my shoulder.

"I just want you to take me." I whispered into his ear.

"Josh, Stefania." Riccardo stood, lifting me in his arms and he rose from his seat. "I believe it is time to depart."

"Yeah, we're heading out too." Josh didn't even bother breaking eye contact with Stefania as he answered. Seems like everyone was on the same page.

I buried my head in his neck, giggling uncontrollably as Riccardo carried me through the club. Stefania and Josh ambled closely behind.

"You can put me down now," I wriggled in his arms as his grip tightened.

"Oh no. You wanted this. So now everyone gets to see that you are dancing with the Devil."

RICCARDO MOANED MY NAME, shuddering as he came hard. I panted beneath him, the echoes of my own climax still humming through my body. An amused grin spread across his mouth as he looked down at me, the sweat on our skin making us slick.

"The way you squeeze my cock when you come, drives me insane. Any control I have evaporates."

"Sweet-talking doesn't earn you a tip." I bit my bottom lip playfully.

"Are you going to try and sneak out like a thief again?" Riccardo grabbed my hands and pulled them above my head, holding me captive.

"Maybe, maybe not. The unpredictability will keep it interesting though so I guess you will find out in the morning." I pushed against his hands but he wasn't relinquishing control. I didn't mind the pressure; it was firm but not threatening.

"What if I don't go to sleep? I might watch you all night."

He bowed his head down and nipped at my glistening shoulder, his teeth grazing my skin.

"Oh, the roofie I slipped you should render you useless soon enough, so the choice will be made for you." My off-the-cuff delivery threatened to be betrayed by the twitching corners of my mouth.

"Alexia, you kill me." Riccardo threw his head back in a full throaty laugh and his body shook above me. "I should chain you to my bed."

"Now you're just teasing me." I batted my eyelashes playfully. "I would have thought you Cassius men didn't need chains though. Can't you just bewitch me into staying?"

He sighed as he released my hands and rolled off of me. "That is the first time I have ever wished that bullshit story was true."

I was disappointed for two reasons, the delicious pressure which he filled me with (even semi-erect) was gone and his playful mood had faltered. I wanted them both back regardless of which came first.

I rolled on top of him, my legs straddling either side of his hips as I whispered suggestively. "Why? So I can provide you with many sons?"

He shook his head as his grin crept back. "No. So I'd have you under my spell."

"And then what would you do with me?" I trailed my fingers along the contours of his chest, my touch teasing the defined walls of muscle.

"Kidnap you. I'd take you somewhere costal so that we could be naked all day and swim in the ocean. The Mediterranean is an almost surreal colour green. It is even more impressive than my family history." Riccardo pulled me down so that I collapsed against his chest.

"Wow, that sounds amazing. You know, I wouldn't have to

be under a spell." I breathed against his neck. "You could ask me and I'd probably say yes."

What's not to love about a beach escape? I adored Rome but being naked with Riccardo by the ocean, that was a very easy sell.

"You would go away with me? Just like that?" Riccardo pulled away from me so he could gauge my reaction.

He had genuinely expected me to say no, I guess given that we had known each other less than 72 hours it would have been a safe bet. What he didn't know was that logic and I weren't exactly besties, which was something that was often pointed out to me.

"For a couple of days, sure why not? I would have to see when I could swing the time off but, yeah, I would go."

Riccardo shook his head in disbelief, "You say that now as a hypothetical but I think in reality you might not be so eager."

"Why is it difficult to believe? If I want to do something I go and do it."

"As I witnessed first hand." He raised his brow sarcastically.

"You know what I mean." I swatted his arm. "I don't want to sit on the sidelines hoping stuff happens. You have to make it happen."

I wasn't one to sit idle, I couldn't. It was a compulsion to move which saw me come to Europe in the first place, the need to explore - knowing there was more to life than studying and work. Adventures and experience were more valuable to me than a mundane routine. It was more than itchy feet. It was about discovery of self and the only way I was going to know what I was capable of was to keep pushing myself out of my comfort zone and stretching my boundaries.

"You are so truly unique, Alexia. I have an excitement when I'm around you that I haven't felt in a very long time."

The warmth of his smile lit up his face; whatever tension had been there had dissolved. I liked that I had that effect on him.

"That's just 'cause I'm *really* good at sucking cock. It's ok... I'm kind of a big deal when it comes to blow jobs."

"Yes, yes you are." Riccardo didn't even try to attempt to hide his grin as his finger traced my collarbone. "And now that I know more information about you, I fully intend to use it to my advantage."

"Is this your way of angling for another blow job?"

"I was referring to your willingness to go away with me, but perhaps in the interim we can continue to investigate the many reasons I get excited around you."

8

Tough Choices

IT WAS easy being with Riccardo. Days turned into weeks and he asked no more of me than I was willing to give. It was probably the most effortless relationship I'd ever had, not that I had a lot to compare it to. Riccardo, Josh and the rest of the Harvard crew filled their days with exploring Rome and all of its majestic glory, no doubt a hardship to endure while the rest of us worked for a living.

Other parts of my life remained largely unchanged. I still worked at the trattoria, I still lived with Stefania and I still lusted after clothes and shoes I couldn't afford. It had been the longest I'd been still in a while and I had started to get that itch. Work bored me and while it was honest if I had to get one more tourist a dish that they couldn't pronounce, I would scream. I wanted more, to do something more meaningful with my days other than refill water glasses and balance food-laden plates.

It wasn't just the mundane mentality of my work that was draining me, although the monotony of it was a major contributing factor, it was the money too. Luigi (our animated boss) was fantastic in allowing us to stay in an apartment he provided but after covering utilities and other living expenses, it didn't leave a lot to play with. I craved something else and being with Riccardo gave me a glimpse of what I could have if I went after it.

Stefania and I would sometimes tag along with Ricardo and co. on their adventures. They were living large and while we were with them we got treated to the spoils of life with an unlimited income. It was a strange experience for me and while Stefania had no issue with Riccardo bank-rolling our extravagant recreational activities, it simmered uncomfortably with me. I knew that what Riccardo was spending was just a drop in the ocean, but I'd never used a man for money. Sex maybe, but never money.

"It's just money Lexi, he has plenty." Stefania would argue whenever I brought it up.

"That's not the point and you know it. His family already thinks I'm a money grabbing parasite. I'm not about to give them more reason to think poorly of me." I argued, knowing it was more about my own personal integrity rather than his family's opinion that plagued me. I could never be a kept woman and no matter what we dressed it up as, that's what I would end up being if we continued long term.

I had the unfortunate pleasure of meeting the Cassius family while attending a family gathering about a week into our relationship. They were all present, well most of them minus the absent brother who'd left the family nest.

Riccardo's mother was immaculately dressed and didn't even try to be humble. She was loud and brassy, her bleached-blonde hair teased within an inch of its life. Predictably she had been less than pleased that Riccardo had taken to dating a waitress and conveyed her displeasure by ignoring me all night.

Riccardo's father attempted civility by smiling and greeting me in English but his pretense fell to the wayside rather quickly when he switched to his native tongue to congratulate his son on the fine piece of ass he was fucking but warned him that bringing her home was bound to upset his mother. Normally I would have responded with a quick witted come-back which would have been peppered with some "fuck you" and "asshole" but I honestly didn't care what this elitist bastard thought of me, he wasn't worth my time. Riccardo of course hadn't shared my sentiment and had launched into a hushed but volatile showdown with his father, and while I appreciated Riccardo going to bat for me it was unnecessary. It had been our objective to piss off his family so as far as I was concerned the frosty reception meant a job well done.

Enzo and Marcus were much of the same; wash, rinse and repeat - rude, obnoxious and judgmental. Their not-so-subtle whisperings conveyed their assumptions that I was looking to either land a rich husband or use Riccardo for a status symbol. I didn't bother to correct their wrongful assumptions. It still amazed me that Riccardo had turned out so well adjusted, he was relatively normal considering the environment he had been raised in.

I assumed Riccardo's original ambition of "ruffling feathers" had been more fun in his theoretical scenario than in the practical application as he spent the rest of the night brooding and angst ridden. This translated into some rather fierce and heated sex later that night, so it was not a complete waste of an evening.

He did however limit our exposure to his family, which confused me a little as I thought the whole idea of our public relationship was to give them the middle finger, but as it wasn't my deal I didn't argue.

The nights were spent together. Regardless of what we

were doing or if I was working or not, I would inevitably end up in his bed. It became a sort of habit and the few times I didn't go to his apartment would see him quietly knocking on my door in the early hours of the morning.

"*Buongiorno Riccardo!*" Stefania's bright cheery voice burst into the room uninvited. She didn't even try to hide her delight at seeing his naked body wrapped around mine, the sheets had fallen off of us throughout the night.

"*Ciao Stefania,*" Riccardo yawned not bothering to be embarrassed as he reached down and retrieved the discarded bedding.

"Go away Stefania!" I groaned into my pillow, shutting my eyes tightly.

"She isn't a morning person." Stefania giggled. She wasn't kidding, I hated mornings.

"Well perhaps she should move in with me so she can be spared the early wake up calls." I felt Riccardo's hand rub my back gently.

"Oooooooo you are trying to steal my Lexi? But I would miss her. Can I move in too?" Stefania nattered excitedly. She had really warmed to Riccardo, being with Josh had certainly helped that but mostly she saw he was a decent guy who gave her no cause to doubt him. So given her new found "friend-ship" with him, I couldn't tell if she was joking or genuinely asking to move in with Riccardo. He had floated the idea of me moving my things to his apartment, arguing I spent so many nights there it made sense. As practical as the offer had seemed it was still a no go for me.

"You know I can hear you both?" I groaned as I tried to hide my head under the pillow.

"So if you can hear me, perhaps you should give my offer some more consideration." Riccardo chuckled in my ear, lightly kissing my back.

"But only if I get to come too!" Stefania added (clearly she hadn't been joking). "I am just grabbing my cardigan, I'm showing Josh the Vatican today and you know how tight-up they get about bare skin in that place." Stefania rustled through the closet before heading back toward the door. "Don't steal Lexi while I'm gone." She blew air kisses as she bounded from the room.

"So?" Riccardo's fingers tip-toed up my back, his voice hopeful.

"You heard Stefania, she would miss me. Besides your place is further from work." I rolled over onto my back and nestled against his warm skin. I didn't want to hurt his feelings but us living together would never happen.

"You could come work for me." Riccardo tilted his head to the side, his eyes gleaming with excitement.

"What? You got a job?" I sat up in bed and hugged him.

I knew he technically didn't *need* a job but I was glad he was going to be doing something more productive than living off his trust fund. He had a masters degree for God's sake. From Harvard. "That's great. What will you be doing?"

"I'm going to work for my father, Alexia. It's time I shared some of the responsibilities with my brothers." He circled his arms around me. "I start Monday and I'm going to need an assistant."

I tried not to be horrified by the prospect of him going into the family business. Honestly, I was surprised. He wasn't like *them* - he was different. He was capable of so much more than being saddled with the legacy of his last name. He could be his own man; surely his brother Nicholas had set a precedent? It seemed that in the last few days I hadn't been the only one who had been considering career choices.

"You can't be serious." I tried to let Riccardo see how disappointed I was. "Firstly, your father hates me so I'm not sure he is going to congratulate you for hiring your *piece of ass* as an assistant and secondly, your *assistant*? Really? We both know why you would want to hire me, so no - I won't work for you." I had no interest in being part of the office scenery or any other *tasks* the job might offer.

"Alexia, did you not express to me the other day that you were bored being a waitress? That you wanted to do something with your degree? I'm giving you a chance to do that. You are more than qualified for the position." His brow knitted in confusion as if he was honestly bewildered about why this was such a bad idea. Maybe he thought I'd have jumped at the opportunity?

"I know what position you are talking about." I levelled him with my icy stare. Being called a whore didn't bother me, but there was no way I was ever going to become one.

"Alexia, I'm not hiring you for sex if that's what you are inferring." Riccardo frowned in disgust.

"That's exactly what it will be. Thanks but no thanks." I slurred sarcastically, wanting to shut the conversation down. It was our first real disagreement and I didn't like the way it made me feel.

"Ok, suit yourself." Riccardo conceded shaking his head, "I was just thinking..."

"Yeah well don't think. I'm more than *qualified* to do that on my own." I snapped, unable to stop the frostiness I was feeling from seeping into my tone.

"Please don't fight with me, *bella*. I was just trying to help." Riccardo tilted my chin, "Look at me. Alexia, you are very capable of doing more than what you are currently doing and I thought I could offer you an alternative. I wasn't trying to offend you. Friends can help friends; it's usually an acceptable process."

My anger spiked. I wasn't sure if it was disappointment in myself or in him. I knew all he was trying to do was help but I also knew how easily it could turn into being controlled. I wouldn't go there, I had told him that at the start. I wouldn't allow myself to change, especially not for a man. "So it's my fault? Look, I know you think you were helping but you aren't. Let it go and if you don't want to fight with me then I suggest you leave."

"Alexia, come on. A simple disagreement and you're kicking me out?" He stared at me in disbelief. I couldn't expect him to get it, after all he barely knew me. We'd been together just over a month?

"Riccardo, just go. I'll talk to you later but right now I'd rather be alone." I pulled my knees up to my chest, wishing he'd just leave. The truth is, it was myself I was most angry with. Being with Riccardo had been easy, I enjoyed his company and I really liked being around him but if I hadn't been embroiled in whatever it was we were doing, I would have moved on a while ago. I was deluding myself into believing I could stay anywhere for too long.

Riccardo let out a long audible breath, "Fine. I'm not the enemy here, just remember that." He stalked off the bed and grabbed his clothes.

I avoided his eyes as he pulled on his jeans, I knew I had probably over reacted but it was too late. Riccardo grabbed his keys from the bedside table. "People fight Alexia, they have disagreements and they move on. I'll speak to you later." He kissed my forehead and quietly walked out the door.

I watched him go, he had been unfairly targeted by my anger and yet I couldn't stop myself. He had never treated me with anything but respect. I needed to get a grip. My boredom was the reason I felt unfulfilled, not because of anything Riccardo had done or not done. The uneasiness I felt was from complacency, I had become too comfortable. It was a feeling I didn't enjoy. It was time to find a new job.

I pushed myself off the bed and grabbed a towel. My objectives today were to have a shower and then to find a new exciting job. The first one was easy, the second might be more difficult but I would scour the city if I had to. I was Lexi Reed and I had the power to shape my own destiny.

9

Changing Lanes

IT HAD TAKEN me most of the day, but I'd finally landed alternative employment. Armed with a hand-written resume and my trademark feisty determination I managed to secure an administration role at a small public relations firm. I suspected my appointment had more to do with my breasts than the fact I had a degree in business (the man who hired me struggled to pull his eyes from my chest during the course of our impromptu interview) but I knew that with my foot in the door, I would prove my worth.

Besides, I was under no delusions. He would fire me just as easily as he had hired me, regardless of his opinion of my rack, if I didn't perform. I was excited; a charge ran through my veins. I had set myself a goal and I had achieved it. I limped home, my feet hurt from roaming the city in heels all day, but I felt good. I would start my new position on Monday, which meant I was only able to give Luigi two days notice that I was leaving my waitressing job. It was unfortunate and made me feel shitty but my new boss was unwilling to hold the position open so I either took it now or I passed, which was not an option. I had no choice but to make my peace with it, I hoped Luigi would understand.

I quickly changed into a pair of shorts and a t-shirt, pulling my hair into a ponytail to get ready for my shift. My feet welcomed the flat sandals that I slid them into, happy to be free of the enclosed pumps I'd been wearing. The casualness of the trattoria was definitely something I would miss but I needed to move on and there was no turning back.

I grabbed my apron and sprinted out the door. I wanted to speak to Luigi before my shift, to explain that I would be leaving. I thought maybe until he found someone to replace me I could work both jobs, my new position was strictly 9-5 weekdays so I could juggle them both until he found someone suitable. It was the decent thing to do. Hopefully he would also allow me to stay at the apartment until I'd scraped together enough for my own place or at least let me pay my portion of the rent so I didn't have to move out. My living arrangements hadn't really factored into my decision but would still have to be dealt with.

"Alessandra. Come, *bella*. Eat before you start." Maria, Luigi's kind-hearted wife and head chef gestured as I entered the kitchen. "I've made a beautiful sauce. You try." She thrust the spoon toward my mouth without giving me a chance to respond.

"Thanks Maria," I gingerly licked the spoon. "Mmmm it's good. Your sauce is always perfect." I smiled. "Is Luigi around? I need to talk to him."

"Yes, Yes of course." Maria threw the used spoon into the sink before stirring her sauce with a huge wooden paddle. "*LUIGI!*" she hollered, "*Cucina!*" She offered him no more information as she summoned him.

Luigi walked in, his face flustered as usual. "You're leaving." He looked at me with sadness in his eyes.

"Yes, I'm sorry. How did you know?" I immediately felt horrible, the last thing I wanted to do was screw him over. He had been so good to me.

He shrugged, "I knew you would go eventually. They all come and then they go. You going home?"

"No, not yet. I found another job." I cringed as I bit my lip, wishing this didn't suck so much. I hadn't expected to feel so horrible about this.

"Alessandra, I'm sorry *bella*. We can't pay you more. This is all I have." Luigi waved his arms around in the direction of the kitchen.

"It's not really the money Luigi, I need to do something else. Grow up a little. I can't be a waitress for the rest of my life. I start Monday, I know that messes things up for you so I'll work nights until you find someone else. I'm sorry. It's just time I go." I needed him to understand that it hadn't been about the money. Sure it was a contributing factor, but more importantly it was me who need the change. More money wouldn't have changed the fact I had felt unsatisfied.

"*Bella*, it's fine. I understand. You're young. You go be happy. If you could stay maybe a week or two? 'Til I get a new girl? That would help me." He rubbed the back of his neck, the deep lines around his eyes crinkling with concern.

"Of course, as long as you need. I'm hoping to stay in the apartment. I know it's a lot to ask but I'll pay rent, just until I get my first regular pay check." I prayed he would allow me to stay, not really having an alternate plan.

"Alessandra you stay as long as you want." His face warmed with kindness. "We work something with the money later. I'm not putting you out on the streets. Maria would kill me." He laughed as his wife playfully swatted him with a tea towel.

"Come," He drew me into a warm embrace. "You've been a good girl. We loved you working here. No be sad, ok?"

I nodded into his chest, a lump forming in my throat. Yeah emotions definitely sucked and I would miss this place and these people.

"Ok. Work now!" Luigi shook my shoulders gently, "Stefania's Americano is here and she is no working. I need someone to take orders. Go." He guided me to the door leading into the main part of the restaurant.

I smiled as I blinked back tears; touched by the kindness this man had shown me in the last couple of months. It had been unparalleled to anything I'd experienced.

Stefania was, as Luigi had described her, twirling her hair and giggling at Josh. He was defying the odds and still held her attention. Seated with him were Riccardo, Thomas and Shawn. I had hoped it was just Josh, even though I knew chances were Riccardo would be with him. It's not like I was avoiding him, I just wasn't ready to admit I had acted like a raving lunatic this morning.

Stefania blew Josh a kiss as I moved closer to the table, "I'll get beer." She turned to me and gave me a quick hug, "Lexi, I haven't seen you all day, I was worried."

"I was just sorting some things out." I smiled as my eyes floated over to Riccardo. He was sitting quietly but I could feel the weight of his stare on me. He had watched me intently since I had walked in.

"Riccardo, have you got a minute?" I figured it was easier to get it over with, I didn't want for the tension to carry throughout the rest of the night.

"Oh-oh! Someone is in the dog house," laughed Thomas and bumped his shoulder against that of his friend.

Riccardo gave Thomas a dark look that silenced him before he turned to me, "Of course Alexia." He stood up and moved away from the table.

"Um, over here." I pulled him to an unoccupied part of the restaurant, we were still in full view of everyone but at least no one could hear us. It was as much privacy as we were going to get given the circumstances.

"Alexia, we don't have to do this now. It's ok, it was just a disagreement."

"No Riccardo, I need to say sorry. I was a complete bitch. I shouldn't have snapped at you. I overreacted. You see, people trying to change or control me, it's like a hot button and I fly off the handle before I think. I know you were trying to help but I saw it as something else. Regardless, I still should have handled it better."

"Alexia, beautiful." Riccardo pulled me closer to him, "I would never try and change you. You are perfect the way you are."

"But I'm not. See that's what I'm trying to tell you. I'm not perfect. I need you to see that." I placed my hands around his face, tilting his chin towards me. I needed him to look at me, see my imperfections.

"I'll only see what's in front of me and until you prove to me otherwise then I will not see any of these flaws of which you speak." His lips hovered above mine threatening to kiss me. He didn't move any closer though.

"I found a job." I blurted out without the benefit of a segue, breaking the moment. "A real job. It's at a small PR firm in the city. They handle some local events, nothing huge but it's a start." I pulled away slightly, giving us some much needed distance.

"That's amazing news. Congratulations! We should be

celebrating." Riccardo's smile broadened. He made no attempt to regain the lost distance between our bodies.

"I feel good about this. It's a good change. I need it." I was not really sure if I was telling him or reaffirming it for myself. I guess either was good.

"I know, I'm happy for you."

"Ok, well I just wanted to say sorry. I need to get back to work." I took a step back not sure what more I should say. I hated that things were weird between us.

"Don't be awkward around me Alexia. I don't think I could stand it if we were no longer friends." He reached out and lightly brushed my arm.

"We're friends. Of course we're friends." I wanted to be friends, he was the first guy in a really long time that had been decent towards me and I really enjoyed being with him. I knew eventually we would end, we both knew that, but I don't think I was ready just yet. I was greedy, I knew it but I wanted him a little longer.

"And will my *friend* be celebrating her new role with me later tonight?" His eyes darkened as he stepped closer.

"Ok."

"You don't sound sure?" His finger traced the line of my jaw, he really had the sexy seduction thing down, I'm not sure I had it in me to say no.

"I want to see you Riccardo." I confirmed, leaving no doubt I wanted him as much as he wanted me.

"Good. Now get back to work, I imagine your days of slacking off are numbered." His hand trailed down my neck and back before it reached my ass, his open palm playfully smacking it.

"Don't start things you won't finish Riccardo." I breathed into his ear "I'm not scared to get a little rough," I teased wanting to get back to an emotion I was comfortable with. It was shallow perhaps, but sex – lust, I was better with dealing with that rather than with weird feelings of expectation.

"Well then, tonight we shall see what I will or will not finish." Riccardo smacked my ass again, a little harder this time. "I'm not scared to get rough either."

10

Drunken Decisions
Three weeks later

"LEXI! Don't interpret what I tell you, just do it like I say!" My new supervisor yelled at me from behind his desk. "I'm not paying you to think, I'm paying you to do. So do!"

I stood there, unflinching. His ranting routine was something I had gotten used to. He was old-school and didn't appreciate my flair. Asshole. I could do his job in my sleep and raise the level of productivity.

"Dom, I just think it would be more cost effective if we did it this way. I have the supporting data if you would just look at it." I lowered the printed spreadsheet in my hand to the desk in front of him.

"You think I give a shit about figures? It's my way or the highway." His face flushed with anger. "I'm doing you a favour. You aren't even supposed to be working here. You only have a holiday visa. It's my ass on the line so lay low, shut up and stop being difficult."

His ass was not on the line, perhaps the owner who had employed me could be liable, but he had made a habit of hiring people on holiday visas. While he still had to pay us a fair rate he was able to dodge taxes and other entitlements. Dom, my not-so-bright superior (and I use that term loosely) was from England and therefore "legal" so despite me being smarter and more qualified than him, he out-ranked me.

"Whatever." I grabbed the spreadsheet off his desk and walked out of his office.

I hated this job. Correction I hated this company, the job itself was awesome but working for these backward fuckwits was draining my soul. I wonder if Luigi would take me back? It had only been three weeks. Maybe the new girl wasn't working out? No! I had to stick it out. Running back to the trattoria was not an option.

I looked at the clock ticking slowly, another fifteen minutes before I could leave. Fifteen more minutes of misery. I needed to drink, heavily.

"Lexi!" Dom screamed from his office. "Get me Michaela on the phone. Some dumb shit forgot to notify the paper of the art fair on this weekend. They've paid for a fucking quarter page ad."

"Dom, the art fair is your account. I reminded you about it last week."

"Oh, so it's my fault? If you reminded me, why didn't you just book the ad? You trying to piss me off? Get her on the phone and fix it."

Fuck my life! If this was an isolated incident perhaps I could deal with it but no, this was an everyday occurrence. Dom fucked up, yelled and then I had to fix it. Any glory was his and his alone.

"I'll fix it." I breathed through clenched teeth. I was going to have to look for another job. Not because I couldn't handle it, 'cause the work load was not a problem but if I spent another couple of weeks here with this asshole I was going to end up in jail, I'm not sure I had enough resources to cover up the murder I was going to commit.

I dialled the friendly classifieds editor, Michaela, and managed to sweet talk the "forgotten" ad into tomorrow's edition despite the deadline having passed an hour ago. I was going to owe her big time.

Ten minutes. Was it possible that time was moving backward? How was fifteen minutes taking so god damn long? I switched off my monitor and grabbed my handbag. Fuck it, I was done for the day. What was he going to do? Fire me? Then who would fix his shit? I was out of the office and down the hall before he had a chance to yell my name again. With any luck he wouldn't even notice I was gone, although this was probably wishful thinking - the man noticed everything when it came to me. He was creepy.

"You're early," Riccardo's mouth curled into a smile, he was relaxed leaning up against his "old" Mercedes. The thing was worth more than my apartment building but he loved driving his toy, not admiring it in a garage. Things of beauty were made to be enjoyed, or so he said.

"I'm done for the day. Dom was riding my ass and I think I'm officially sick of hearing my name. What are you doing here?"

"I thought you might like a ride. I haven't seen you in a few days. I'm sorry you've had a horrible day. I can make it better."

It hadn't been a conscious effort but Riccardo and I had drifted in the last couple of weeks. I still wanted him and he wanted me and when we were together it was explosive but deep down I knew I shouldn't be with him. I wanted to let him go, knowing we had no future together but he was such an amazing man I found myself selfishly going back. At least neither of us loved each other; that meant there was no shame in enjoying each other's company if no one was going to get hurt. Despite my limited availability he never complained and took me as I was. This had been a rare find and I wanted to enjoy it for as long as I could, knowing that not all men would be as understanding.

"Riccardo, I'm in a really bad mood. I'm talking epic bitchiness. Do yourself a favour, you don't want to be around me right now." I felt compelled to warn him.

I respected him too much to intentionally be cruel and I knew what I was capable of when I got in one of my moods. I didn't want to subject him to that although the release he would give me would probably improve my disposition. It was a double-edged sword.

"Alexia, I can handle your moods."

"Ok, you've been warned. I gave you your out. We have to hang out at my apartment though. Stefania is still depressed Josh left last week and I promised we would get very drunk." Silently I was relieved that he wasn't deterred by my caution. I had missed him and wanted him in my bed, feeling him pulse as I came around his cock. Yeah, I definitely needed to have sex.

"I don't mind. We can pick up some dinner and wine on the way back to your apartment." Riccardo opened the door he had been leaning against. I loved that he was so accommodating, so easy to be around.

"Oh wine isn't going to cut it. We're going to need hard liquor. If you can find some of the epic Grappa we had the night your friends went back to the States that would be even better." I pressed my body against him, kissing his lips as I breathed him in. My body melted against his, he responded by pulling me closer.

"That I can definitely do." He smiled as he reluctantly pulled away and beckoned me into the car. He watched as I slid into the seat before he moved across to the driver side of his prized Gullwing. He started the car and we purred out into traffic, weaving through the narrow streets of Rome.

After a few pit stops to acquire the aforementioned food and Grappa (a home-distilled beverage that was around 60% alcohol and tasted like rocket fuel) we made our way back to the apartment I shared with Stefania.

"Oh, you brought company." Stefania not so subtly displayed her displeasure. She was sitting cross-legged in front of the television watching some mindless over-acted soap, it had been her usual pastime for the last few days.

"I promise I won't cramp your style." Riccardo offered as he placed the food on the coffee table in front of her.

"Stefania, be nice. I have had the most crap-tastic day and I really don't want to have to run interference between the two of you." I joined her on the floor, balancing the all-important bottles of highly-potent alcohol.

"You don't have to run interference between us, we're friends aren't we Stefania?"

"Of course we are friends," Stefania smirked. "Let's get really drunk then maybe I can be your *special* friend like Lexi is."

"Ok, did you start drinking without me?" I noticed a half-empty bottle of cheap wine sitting on the floor beside the coffee table.

"Maybe. Don't umpire me." Stefania crossed her arms, tipping her chin in the opposite direction and had she not smiled she would have probably convinced me she was annoyed.

"It's *judge* and I'm not." I pulled out the takeaway containers and peeled away their lids. If I had any chance of stopping Stefania from humping Riccardo's leg, I was going to have to get her to eat something.

"So this mood you're in, is it about Josh leaving or your lack of sex?" I asked cautiously.

"Both. I think I'm swearing off men for a while." Stefania sighed dramatically. "Yes, that's the answer. From now on only women."

"Yet only a minute ago you were angling to sleep with Riccardo." I gestured to Riccardo who was watching our conversation with interest.

Nothing we said really surprised him anymore, he had been initiated into Stefania's brand of crazy and he knew of her penchant for women so the topic at hand was not entirely out of left field.

"Sweetie, I love you but we both know you aren't going to stop sleeping with men."

"I would if you would sleep with me. I've heard the two of you through the wall and it's hot. I know I could make you come Lexi, come hard." If I had any doubts about how much she had been drinking, they were well and truly in the past. We were back to this old chestnut about why I wasn't cool with licking pussy. It was going to be a long ass night.

"As flattering as that is, I don't think how many times you can make me come would solve this issue."

"Why did you never want to sleep with me?" Stefania blurted out. "I mean I know you like guys but I'm pretty right?" She'd look so vulnerable, needing reassurance that my rejection of her sexual advances was not because she wasn't good enough.

"Stefania, I'm just not into girls. It's nothing personal. I just prefer dick." I gave her a hug of affirmation.

"But how do you know unless you try?" She said with absolute seriousness. "I bet you I could go down on you better than *he* could." She pointed to Riccardo who was passively still standing beside us, no doubt enjoying the show.

"Why don't I get some plates then. You ladies seem to have everything under control here." He smirked as he strode out of the lounge-room.

"So is it me or him you are trying to impress?" I rolled my eyes as I popped the cap off the bottle and took a swig of the Grappa. I figured this was a conversation best had while drinking.

"I'm just saying you can't *know* what you don't *know*." Stefania grabbed the bottle from my hands and helped herself to a drink.

"That makes no sense." I took the bottle from her and again pressed it to my lips, allowing the burning liquid to slide down my throat.

Stefania's attraction toward me was nothing new, for the most part it was playful flirting and despite the context didn't make me uncomfortable. Tonight was different though, it was almost as if she needed me. I wondered if she was right, if it was something I could do, if us being together would comfort her in some way. My mind fogged with a jumble of thoughts, was I actually considering sleeping with her? Was it alcohol or was it the friendship I had for this beautiful girl who had become such a major part of my life that made the idea no longer seem so absurd?

Riccardo re-entered the room carrying some plates, cutlery and glasses he had retrieved from the kitchen. He didn't even try to hide the amused look he had on his face.

"What?" I took the plates from his hand, placing them on the coffee table before he spooned out some of the roasted vegetables on to them.

"I didn't say anything." He shrugged as he joined us on the floor and divided up the grilled beef onto the plates.

"You were thinking it." I didn't need to be a psychic to

know what thoughts were playing on his mind. The same thoughts that were currently on mine.

"I was just thinking that maybe she had a point." He smiled as he handed Stefania some cutlery.

"See! He agrees with me. I knew there was a reason I liked him." Stefania beamed excitedly, taking his words as an endorsement.

"Well then why don't the two of you sleep with each other then?" I lifted the bottle again and took another swig, my buzz increasing. Strangely the thought of the two of them together didn't make me feel weird. I knew I probably should be jealous but whether it was the alcohol or I'd just finally lost my mind, I wasn't.

"I don't think it's me she wants, Alexia." Riccardo took the bottle from my hands and poured us each a very large glass.

"You know encouraging her isn't helping." I picked up my fork and stabbed at my dinner, I could feel the heat from the Grappa coursing through my veins. The floating idea of us, the three of us, being together became more and more like something I actually wanted to do. Maybe it was experimentation or maybe I just really like these two beautiful people who were with me and I wanted to share myself intimately.

"Alexia, I don't believe anything I or anyone else says will change what you decide you do." Riccardo rolled his glass slowly in his palm. "But I understand her desire for you."

He looked so sexy, sitting across from me; the way his mouth moved when he spoke, the way his eyes fired when they looked at me. His dark hair was begging for my hands to run through it. I dropped my fork and crawled over to him. He watched me curiously as I climbed into his lap and pulled his face to mine.

"Do you desire me right now?" I breathed into his mouth.

"Yes." He swallowed slowly, "I always desire you."

I kissed him, hard, not caring that Stefania was sitting across from us. The thought of her watching somehow made it more appealing. Riccardo palmed my ass as I wrapped my legs around his waist. His tongue probed my mouth as he moved his hands across my body.

"Are you trying to tease me?" Stefania groaned from behind me. "Because that just isn't fair."

"Do you want me too?" I turned my head to look at her, not entirely sure what I was saying. Could we still be friends if we did this? Would things ever be the same? This should have been a well thought out decision not some spur of the moment choice but it was like I had given up control, my body was responding on autopilot before my brain had a chance to react.

"I've wanted you for a long time," Stefania crawled over to where Riccardo and I sat.

Without saying a word I reached over and touched her face, her lips kissed my palm as she moved closer to me. It didn't feel as strange as I would have thought, having a woman touch me. I leant into her, allowing my mouth to brush against hers. She responded by opening her mouth and gently sliding her tongue inside. It was nothing like when I kissed Riccardo; in fact it was like nothing I had ever experienced. It was tender and unassuming.

Riccardo kissed my neck while Stefania stayed at my lips. Her hand wandered to my breast, her fingers rolled my nipple and it hardened under her touch. Riccardo's hands moved to the front of my shirt, his fingers slowly unbuttoning it, his touch igniting my skin.

"Alexia," Riccardo stripped the fabric from my torso, I felt his cock harden as he rocked against me.

"Lexi," Stefania moaned as she unhooked my bra, her mouth moving over my skin.

Riccardo lifted me off his lap, his mouth took over my lips

as Stefania's tongue trailed up my breast. My body responded to their touch.

"Do you want this Alexia?" His voice rumbled. "Me here with you? With both of you?" His eyes heated with lust but he was holding back.

Our relationship had started rather unconventionally and it had been largely based on sex, but despite this we had been monogamous. It wasn't something we'd spoken about, it just happened that way. The two of us satisfying each other's needs, there had been no reason for others. I saw in his eyes that he was torn by what I was asking of him. He wanted it, to be with us but I could tell that he was worried that it was some kind of test. Maybe it was a test or maybe it was because I didn't love him that it made it ok. I cared for him and I loved being with him but I didn't love him. There was no way I could ever share a man I loved, so in a way, asking him to do this was more about testing myself than testing him.

"Yes." The word slipped from my lips. It felt right, being there with both of them. I wanted this.

As Riccardo pulled me to my feet Stefania let out a groan of protest at being separated from us.

"Not on the floor." He took my hand and kissed it. Stefania looked at him, smiling approvingly as he took her hand and guided us both to my bedroom.

He lowered me onto the bed, Stefania finding her place by my side. He stepped off the mattress and slowly stripped off his clothing, our eager eyes consuming his naked skin. He was beautiful.

He didn't hesitate as he strode back toward us, his hands moving across my body as they removed my skirt and panties. Stefania joined us, shucking her own clothes. He watched her but didn't touch her, seeming to be fighting an internal war as to whether or not he should follow through with this.

"It's okay Riccardo, I want this." I tried to take the doubt from him.

"I could just watch." He offered slowly kissing me.

"Touch me," I begged; my skin tingled needing the connection.

It was all I needed to say as a tangle of hands and mouths descended on my body, touching me, caressing and kissing me. I felt myself flood as I became more aroused than I'd ever been, every inch of me was stimulated as they both licked and sucked.

I couldn't breathe as Riccardo reached for a condom, I was so worked up and I needed him inside of me. I wanted to feel him fill me.

"Yes," I moaned as I felt him enter me, the sensation of hands and lips all over me threatening to make we come with his one thrust.

I moved against them, allowing them both free reign over my body. I trusted them as they took turns in bringing me to the brink, my body craving its finish. I shattered around them, every inch of my body spent as I sagged into them, spent, stated and slightly overwhelmed.

"Sleep, *bella*," Riccardo whispered in my ear as he pulled me into his arms, Stefania curled up beside me.

I had no energy to fight the fatigue. My body was limp as it lay on the mattress. I couldn't even speak, the energy needed to move my mouth proved to be more than I could muster. Whether it was the alcohol, the emotions of the day or the events of the evening, I couldn't keep my eyes open as sleep began to take me. My lids closed and I floated into unconsciousness, wrapped in the warmth of both of their bodies.

11

Unravelled

I WOKE up feeling unbelievably hot and surrounded by a sea of arms and legs. The reality of the night before was now staring me smack, bang in the face. At some point in the evening I had decided it had been a good idea to have a threesome, sharing myself with the man that was my quasi-boyfriend and the woman who had become my closest friend while living in Rome.

I wasn't sure what I felt as I slowly unwrapped myself from the tangle and moved off the bed.

"Coffee," groaned Stefania as she rolled into the foetal position, obviously not ready to face the day.

Riccardo stretched beside her, his eyes sliding open as he breathed deeply. The morning sun danced across his muscular torso as the light streamed into the bedroom.

"I'll get it if you want to go back to sleep," his voice was husky as he slowly rose to his feet.

"It's fine, I was hot laying in bed." I walked to my closet and pulled out a t-shirt.

He followed, wrapping his arms around me. "Alexia, about last night..."

I shrugged, "Riccardo, there doesn't need to be a conversation. It happened. We were all consenting adults. It's not a big deal."

He looked over at Stefania who was sleeping again. "It's not what I had planned."

"So we improvised. It's a non-issue. That doesn't mean I want to move it into rotation." I reached down and fished out my panties.

"So we're fine?" He looked sceptical as he raised his hand to my face.

"We're fine." I uttered giving him a weak smile.

"Ok, let me go get you breakfast, I'm surprised you aren't nursing a horrible hangover." He reached for his jeans and pulled them on. Underwear was optional today, I guess given the night we'd just had going commando was not a big deal.

I slid on a skirt while he finished getting dressed. Despite what I had said, the vibe between us was different.

"I'll be back," Riccardo kissed me, his eyes clouded.

"It's ok," I tried to reassure him, knowing I was lying though my teeth.

He walked out the bedroom and I heard the front door close. My eyes floated back to Stefania's naked body curled up in my sheets. Last night had probably not been my wisest choice but it was one I was going to have to deal with.

"Stefania," I sat back down on the mattress and shook her. "Stefania wake up."

"Five more minutes," she mumbled, trying to scoot herself further away from me.

"No, wake up now. We need to talk." I figured it was best to get the conversation done sooner than later.

"Ugh," Stefania mumbled. "Ok, Ok." She rolled over onto her back to face me. "Hey." She squinted as her eyes focused. "I had the weirdest dream last night. You are going to laugh so hard when I tell you but we..."

"It wasn't a dream." I cut her off knowing what she was going to say.

"Huh? Me, you and Riccardo?" Stefania looked around and noticed she was naked in my bed. "It actually happened?"

"Yeah. It did."

"Do you hate me now?" Stefania's eyes saddened as she pulled the sheets up to cover herself.

"Why would I hate you? You didn't force me to do anything." Whatever the fall out would be it was not Stefania's fault, I had been in the driver's seat last night.

"But I slept with your boyfriend and lord knows what else I did." Her eyes were wide with confusion, perhaps she had consumed more than just half that bottle of wine before we had arrived home. She appeared to have little recollection of anything that had transpired.

"You blew him, he only had sex with me. It's ok Stefania." I tried to reassure her, ignoring how bizarre it sounded that I was comforting my friend for having had oral sex with my boyfriend.

"And... you are ok with that?" Stefania squeaked. "What about what I did to you?"

"It is what it is, I guess I'm ok with it. Either way, I'm not blaming you for what happened. As for what you did to me, I let you do those things. I wasn't forced and I could have stopped you at any time. If anything I took advantage of you, 'cause clearly you have no recollection of it."

"Where is Riccardo?" Stefania looked around the room, noticing one of the members of our *party* was no longer present.

"He's gone to get breakfast, he'll be back." I explained knowing when he returned shit was bound to get awkward.

"Does *he* hate me?" She winced, pulled her knees protectively to her chest.

"No, of course not. No one hates you." I pulled lightly on her arm, not understanding why she would think anyone would hate her.

"Lexi, I know you keep saying it's not my fault but it wouldn't have happened without me. Things are going to be bad. I am such a dumb person." She shook her head, her face distraught.

"You aren't a dumb person. Stefania we all had choices last night." I couldn't understand why she was beating herself up about it. If anyone one was to blame it was me.

"I took the one friendship I treasured and I fucked it up for sex." Stefania's eyes watered, "Lexi, yes I wanted you. You are beautiful. Of course I wanted you but I didn't want to screw up what we had by sleeping with you." She covered her face with her hands and started to cry, her chest heaving with each sob.

"You haven't screwed it up, we are still friends." I shifted closer to her and put my arm around her shoulders. "Although next time you ask, the answer is going to be no." I tried to laugh, not sure anything I was going to say was going to lighten the situation.

"I need to go," Stefania nodded. "I need to just go for a few days." She attempted to wipe her eyes despite the tears still streaming.

"Go where? Why? Because of what happened?" I pulled away from her in surprise. This was not how I had expected her to react.

"Yes, I don't want to be here when he gets back." She

sobbed, her arms wrapped tightly around her body. She looked so fragile and scared and the fact that I was responsible for that tore me up.

"Stefania," I tried to reason. I just needed her to stay, for the three of us to talk it out and see that everyone was ok. No one needed to feel bad about it. We didn't break any rules. We did nothing wrong. I needed to find a way to show her. Riccardo would help me, I'm sure he would.

"No Lexi, please just let me go. Be with him. Just him. I'll come back in a few days when things calm down. I'm sorry." She hugged me tightly, her eyes damp from tears that seemed to have no end.

She raced from my room and into her own. She was dressed and out the door before I had a chance to convince her to stay. Our harmless night no longer seemed so harmless.

The front door opened, the smell of freshly brewed coffee wafted into the apartment.

"Hey, was that Stefania I saw running out of here?" Riccardo called from the lounge-room.

"Yeah," I mumbled as I ambled out of my room and into the living area. "Things aren't as ok as I thought."

"I'm sorry," Riccardo drew me into his arms. "I should have stopped it."

"Why is everyone apologizing to me? I wanted it to happen." I was so confused. I had wanted this hadn't I? I was ok with it. No one's feelings were supposed to get hurt. How could it all have been so clear to me last night and now things were so skewed.

"You were intoxicated beautiful, I'm not sure you would have made the same choice if you were sober." He brushed the hair away from my face, his voice so apologetic it made me feel even worse.

"What about you? Do you regret it?" I wasn't sure I wanted to know the answer but I couldn't help asking the question.

"Alexia, that is a really hard question for me to answer. I could never regret a night with you, no matter what the circumstances were. I would do anything to make you happy. You've been withdrawn lately. I know you've been miserable or bored and if doing this was going to give you that spark back, then I was willing to try. I miss it so much." He gently kissed my forehead. "But I do wish I could change it, have tried something else."

"I should go home. I think I need to leave Rome." I had made such a mess of things; going back to Australia seemed like the only sensible thing to do. It was time I grew up, accepted that I needed to be a responsible member of society. Get a job, a real job. I couldn't live like I was on vacation forever.

"Alexia, no." Riccardo tilted my chin so I met his eyes. "Don't leave, stay in Rome. Stay with me. We'll find a way for you to be happy. We'll find you a better job. You can be happy here."

"Riccardo, the reason I have such a shitty job is because I don't have a visa. I can't stay." I had been putting off the inevitable. I had originally come to Europe as an escape, for an adventure. I had settled in Rome by pure chance. It was never going to be long term and as wonderful as it had been, I had been on borrowed time for a while.

"So marry me. You won't need a visa, you can stay as long as you like." Riccardo responded with no hesitation.

At first I thought he must be joking, people say things like that all the time but the look on his face told me he was serious. He would actually marry me so I could stay in Rome? There is no way I would allow him to do that. Regardless of whether it was a marriage of convenience or not, I could never make that kind of commitment to someone. What kind of person would that make me? Probably the same kind of person who has a threesome with her boyfriend and her friend and then expects everyone to do a post mortem over pancakes the next morning. I really was a nice piece of work. Kudos Lexi, take a bow. You have reached a new low.

"I can't just marry you so I can work here Riccardo, that's crazy. I can't use you like that. I'm not completely unscrupulous."

"You wouldn't be using me. Alexia, I have the means to make you stay, I want you to stay." Riccardo tried to rationalize.

That just made it worse, that he would want to do something as pathetic as entering a loveless marriage to keep me in Rome. What had I done to him? The whole time Stefania warned me about him and his evil family and it should have been the other way around.

"I can't, I don't...I'm so fucking confused." My head screamed with a torrent of emotions. Shit had gotten beyond messed up and I wasn't going to fix it by making another mistake. I needed to think.

"Just think about it. I promise I won't pressure you." He held me tenderly, showing me much more kindness than I deserved. "The marriage will not change things between us. I won't ever limit you. It is a solution. You don't have to go."

"I'll think about it." I responded numbly, not knowing what else to say.

"That's all I ask. Do you want me to go, to give you some space?" He held me close as he gave me a warm smile.

"Yes. I think it would be for the best." I nodded into his chest, the pain I had caused the two people I cared about was tearing me apart.

"Alexia, please consider my offer. I'll give you all the time you need." He kissed my lips, his fingertips lightly brushing my cheek.

He pulled himself away from me, turning to walk out the door. He paused on the threshold. "I'll see you in a few days."

I waved and gave him a smile. In my heart I knew it was the last time I'd see him. I had to say goodbye. I had prolonged it too long, over-stayed my welcome. He had been so kind and treated me much better than I had ever been treated and that had made me reluctant to leave. But, it was time. The door behind him closed and I felt a deep, deep sadness. I hated good-byes, which is why it was best to not say them. He would forget about me, move on with his life and find someone more suitable, someone his family would accept and someone whom he could love, someone who would love him back. I could never be that person.

I slowly ambled back into my room and pulled out my suit-case that had sat discarded under my bed for months. I had enough saved for a ticket home, granted it would pretty much clean me out but it's what I would have to do. My beautiful friend Emma would surely allow me to stay with her until I got back onto my feet. We'd known each other since high school, her purity of spirit never judged me and despite my constant jet-setting she'd always welcomed me as if no time had passed at all.

I picked up the phone and dialled, waiting for the beep of the international connection.

"Hello," Emma's cheery voice filled my ear. I hadn't real-ized how much I'd missed her till I heard her speak. It was the first time since I had been away that I had been homesick.

"Hey Emz, It's Lexi." I smiled into the phone, knowing that this was the right thing to do. "I've missed you."

"Lexi! Oh my God! I'm so glad you called. I have missed you too!" Emma laughed into the phone excitedly. "What adventure are you up to now? Are you still in Rome? Tell me, I want to hear it all."

My heart warmed with her love and her acceptance, helping to make my decision easier. "And I can't wait to tell you. Can you pick me up from the airport in a day or two? I'm coming home."

12

Stefania

"LEXI!" I called out from the front door, hoping the few days I had been gone would made things easier. It upset me to think that because of one stupid night, she would hate me.

"Lexi," I sang out again as I walked into our apartment. Strangely she hadn't answered, I hoped she still wasn't mad. Maybe she was sleeping or with Riccardo, though it had crossed my mind that they may have broken up over what had happened. Even though Lexi swore she was ok with us being together there aren't many women who can handle that kind of mental baggage. We had been so stupid. You had threesomes with randoms, people you weren't going to see again, not people that you loved.

I wandered through the living-room and into her bedroom; the door had been left open. I peered inside, noticing her bed was made and the room was empty. There was something different about her room. It was so clean and tidy, not even a stray shoe on the floor. Odd.

My feet moved me further into the room as my eyes scanned the space. It looked empty, bare, uninhabited. No. I had to be mistaken. I pulled open the closest and drawers looking for evidence that the room was still lived in but the vacant spaces confirmed what I had suspected. She was gone. Lexi had left.

I slumped onto her bed, my heart heavy with sadness and I noticed a piece of paper that had sat on her bed waiting to be read. She had left a note. I wanted to cry knowing they would be her last words to me.

STEFANIA,

I'm sorry I didn't get to say a proper goodbye. I suck at them and honestly I wasn't sure when you would come back. I'm sorry things got so messed up between us that you felt you had to leave but please know that I adore you and could never hate you.

My leaving has nothing to do with you or the night we spent together. It was just time for me to go home. I have been living in a marvellous fantasy world with you and while it has been some of the most amazing months of my life, even fantasies eventually have to end. I need to be something, do something with my life.

I'm going to try and get a job in PR, a real job not like the second-rate operation I was working for here. I want to find a firm who can take me places. Who knows maybe someday I could have my own business. I know I could be good at it, I know that there is more to me than what I have become.

Please know I have cherished every day with you, working together and living together and I hope you understand why it was time for me to leave. I promise one day to come back, we are going to look at this and laugh. I might even let you kiss me again :) I also now know with 100% certainty that I prefer cock so the next time someone asks me I can answer the question definitively.

Please tell Riccardo I'm sorry. I couldn't stay and I hope that he has a good life. He is such a good man, one who is deserving of a good woman. I hope he finds her someday. Tell him to tell his family to go fuck themselves and not to let their evil change who he is. He is so much more than they could ever be.

I have to go, I need to catch a flight but I have left you some money (sorry it's not much) to cover my part of the rent for the month. I know Luigi said he didn't want my money but I need him to take it. It will make me feel like less of an asshole.

There is so much more I want to say but there isn't time. Sorry.

Goodbye,

Lexi xx

I COULDN'T STOP the tears from falling, knowing she was gone. I hugged the letter close to my heart, knowing it was the only connection I had left of her. I felt lost.

"Alexia? Stefania?" Riccardo called from the living room. "You left your door open. I know this is a safe neighbourhood but you shouldn't leave it unlocked." I heard his footsteps echo through the hall.

I swallowed hard knowing what I was going to have to tell him; that Lexi had left us both.

"In here," I croaked, my voice breaking under the weight of my sadness.

"Stefania?" Riccardo raced into the room. "Are you ok? Are you hurt?" He scanned me for any signs of injury. "Is it Alexia?" He looked around the room seeking an answer as to why I was falling apart.

"She's gone." I sniffed, unable to give him much more in the way of an explanation.

"What do you mean she's gone? She moved out? Where did she go?" Riccardo shook me gently, his voice agitated as he tried to reconcile what I saying. I could see in his eyes that he didn't understand the words coming from my mouth.

"No, she's gone, gone. She left Rome. She went home." I clarified, wishing it was someone else who had to tell him. I knew that they didn't have a conventional relationship but I could tell how much he cared for her. No matter how good the sex was men didn't stay where they weren't happy and for better or worse, Lexi made him smile.

"No. You must be mistaken. She wouldn't just leave." He shook his head viciously, not willing to accept the notion that she had gone. Maybe he, like me, had assumed that after a few days we'd somehow find our way to normalcy.

"She did. She left a letter." I showed him the note I had been clutching tightly to my chest, smoothing out the rumpled page so he was able to read her pretty cursive writing.

Riccardo took the paper from my hands and I couldn't help watch as his eyes followed the script. His face contorted as he received the confirmation he required. His pain was visible.

"How could she just leave?" He roared in anger. "I loved her!"

He picked up a lamp from the bedside table and threw it across the room. The light blub shattered into a million pieces.

"What?" I vacantly responded, not sure I had heard him correctly. "You loved her?" Lexi had spoken of her affection for Riccardo but she had never spoken of love declarations. She would have mentioned something like that, I know she would have and she certainly wouldn't have walked away from someone she loved.

"Yes, I loved her. I asked her to marry me. I asked her to

stay in Roma." Riccardo raked his hair in frustration, his face a mixture of pain and torment.

"Did you tell her you loved her?" I squeaked, not wanting to anger him further. He had already thrown the lamp and although I knew he wouldn't hurt me, he was volatile and I wasn't willing to push my luck.

"No, I didn't want to scare her off. I thought when I proposed she would put it together. I thought I had more time." He squeezed the bridge of his nose, his jaw so tightly clenched the words barely came out.

"But if you loved her, why did we...? You know." I shifted uncomfortably, realizing that it was the first time I had seen Riccardo since we had been intimate with each other.

He opened his eyes and looked at me, his voice no longer filled with anger. "Because I wanted to make her happy. God, I would have cut off my own arm if I knew it would have pleased her." He was living his own version of hell.

"You should have told her, she didn't know Riccardo. She always thought you would eventually find someone else," I tried to rationalize. Lexi wouldn't have left if she knew how he felt. She was a lot of things but she was not uncaring. She would have assumed that Riccardo would have just moved on.

"I didn't want anyone else." Riccardo murmured softly, "I don't want anyone else."

"Then go get her. Find her. There can't be that many Lexi Reeds in one city. Use some of that fancy money you have and get her back. Tell her how much she means to you." I pushed him gently in the chest. He could hop on a plane and find her. He could explain how much she meant to him, she would come back. She wouldn't be too hard to find. A little digging, he could use his family's connections and he'd probably have a phone number and address by tomorrow.

"You think that would change anything? She left." He sunk

onto the bed, defeated. "She walked out the door. She doesn't feel the same way. Am I supposed to go beg? Drag her back so she can be miserable with me? Deep down I knew that she wasn't mine to keep. I knew that we weren't forever but I couldn't stop myself from falling for her." He shook his head in disbelief.

"Riccardo, I'm sorry. I loved her too." I sat down beside him, wrapping an arm around his big broad shoulders. We had been united by the common grief of losing someone we loved.

"I know. Maybe we should start a support group." Riccardo tried to smile but failed, his idea not too far off the mark.

"Do you think she'll ever come back? She said she would one day come back." I tried to sound hopeful, not willing to believe I'd never see her again. Even if it was just one more time, I wanted the opportunity to say a proper goodbye.

"I don't know Stefania. I hope that she does and when she comes back, she is happy." Riccardo stared vacantly off into the distance.

We sat on her bed for what seemed like forever, it was as if she had died; unfairly ripped from our lives suddenly. I cried a little more and Riccardo held me. He didn't say anything else but I knew it had to be worse for him and there was nothing I could say that would make it easier. I wanted to be mad at her, mad for leaving us both. I felt deserted but I couldn't hate her. I just hoped that she found whatever it was she needed to make her happy and that one day she would come back.

13

Home Sweet Home

"LEXI," Emma called from the doorway. "You want something to eat? This jetlag is kicking your ass."

"I'm ok, just hard to get back on Melbourne time. Thanks for asking." I smiled as I unfurled my body and stretched. I hadn't meant to fall asleep on the couch, the mindless TV I had been watching had sapped my ability to remain conscious.

Emma had been generously housing me since my unexpected return home. I arrived at Melbourne International Airport with a suitcase full of clothes and about a hundred dollars in cash. Sadly, I was going to need to rely on her kindness for a little longer at least until I got a job. Not that she ever complained, her beautiful, sunny disposition just wrapped me up in a big blanket of love and said she was happy to have me.

"Have you called him?" Emma said quietly as she sat beside me.

"No, it's better this way. He is probably thanking his lucky stars I'm gone." I smiled.

I had told Emma all about Riccardo and Stefania and my fucked up decision. She never judged me (although I wouldn't blame her if she did) and listened patiently while I recounted the whole sordid tale. When I was done, she simply smiled and asked if I was ok and if I needed anything. That was Emma, no matter what craziness I threw at her, she took it in her stride and loved me anyway. I thank whatever force brought her into my world, knowing deep down I didn't deserve her.

"You are too hard on yourself." She wrapped her arm around my shoulder and squeezed me into a hug. "But I'm not going to tell you what to do. Only Lexi knows what's best for Lexi." She pulled my face to her cheek.

"Stop," I forced a smile. "You will make me cry and you know how much I hate to cry." I blinked away the tears, not sure what emotion I was fielding today. It really could be anything.

"No tears!" Emma squeezed me before tactfully changing the subject. "Oh hey. Have you heard the new Power Station album? It came out last week. It is so good. James sounds amazing!"

"No, I didn't get it yet. I can't wait to hear it." I was genuinely excited, Emma mentioned the only thing that was guaranteed to pull me from my funk. We loved the band Power Station, we had innocently stumbled across them on the Internet and despite them being nobodies from New York we had become avid fans. We followed their steady rise, excited to see the band progress. They had just recently landed a contract with a major record label and were about to embark on their first stadium show tour. Our early support had made us feel somewhat responsible for their success. We adored them, probably a little bit more than just adored but they were so talented and good looking, it was bound to happen.

"Is there a video yet? I am so glad they finally got a deal.

The minute I get a job we are flying somewhere to see a show."
I was actually excited about something for the first time in days.
"Alex Stone is so good looking, the things I would do to him if I
ever met him."

I wasn't kidding either. That man did things to me inter-
nally I couldn't describe. I knew the chances of my meeting
him and therefore sleeping with him were less than remote but
it didn't mean I couldn't fantasize about him, and he factored
heavily in my fantasies. Thanks to his Scandinavian heritage
and a wicked win in the gene lottery, Alex Stone was a blue
eyed, blonde, six-foot-four sex god. I'm not even kidding,
panties disintegrated in his vicinity. He just had to give you his
beautiful twisted grin and you would most likely cream your
pants. Rumour was, he knew it and he was rarely short of
female company. Not that I blamed him.

"Lexi!" Emma shook her head. "I just think it would be
awesome to see them up close. You know?"

"Yes seeing them would be pretty cool but I still maintain
sleeping with Alex would be better." I smirked, thinking we
should probably jump on YouTube so I could continue my
mental debasement with the help of a visual aid.

"Ok, well now that we've got a smile on your face, lets get
you job hunting. There is a small PR firm in the city that's
looking for someone. Nothing huge but it's a foot in the indus-
try. Besides, it couldn't be worse than those horrible people you
worked for in Rome." Emma handed me a copy of the employment classifieds.

I accepted the newspaper and gave Emma a big hug.
Unable to express the gratitude I felt, it was the best I could
offer. "Thanks for everything."

"Hey, it's in my interest to get you working. You
promised that once you got a job we would go see Power
Station in a stadium so I'm going to do everything I can to

make sure that happens!" Emma giggled as she returned my hug.

It wasn't going to be easy moving on from Riccardo. The guilt I felt from running away still tormented me but deep down I knew it was the right thing to do. I didn't love him and we'd be stuck in a limbo that I knew neither of us would break. Inevitably, I would have hurt him and he deserved better than that. By me leaving, I set us both free. He could find someone who he could fall in love with, plan a future with, someone who was everything he deserved. Walking away was the first decent thing I had done in a long, long time and for that I was proud of myself. I hoped one day I would return to Rome, see him again, and explain why I had left. I just hoped that enough time would pass so that he didn't hate me. He would probably be married to some kick-ass Italian wife and have a soccer team of kids (probably all boys) and he would barely remember who I was.

As for Stefania, something in my gut told me that Riccardo would make sure she was ok. She would no doubt be back to her usual effervescent self in no time, flirting with tourists in *Luigi's Trattoria*. Riccardo would check in on her and make sure she didn't go too far off the rails, they had become friends in their own right since we had started dating and I hoped that it would continue, even in my absence. Someday Stefania would find some guy (or girl) that was worthy of her and she'd probably settle down too. Who knows? Maybe they'd end up a couple. Stranger things could happen. I knew that they would be ok, it just sucked that we couldn't be ok together.

For now, this is where I belonged, broke and unemployed but with my integrity intact. I would be ok, I was excited about the prospects in front of me and I was looking forward to finally using the degree I had worked so hard to get. While being with a man hadn't broken me this time, it had stirred up feelings inside me that I wasn't comfortable with. The guilt, the emotion, the highs and the lows, these were things that were better avoided in the future. It had been proven I wasn't the type of girl who could do relationships (even fake ones), my track record spoke for itself.

There was an easy calm with accepting what I viewed my fate to be. I would never give my heart so there was no need for the pretense. Instead I would focus on myself, be the best version I could be and allow myself to enjoy men purely for the pleasure they could provide. It was a good plan; there was no need for anything else. Unless you counted the fantasies of Alex Stone twisting through my mind, after all, how much trouble could I get into with a fantasy?

Chapter 1

Reed, Lexi Reed

"REED. MY office. *NOW*."

Crap. The fact that she was yelling to me from her office was a sure sign that Kate was fuming. I did a quick mental stocktake of the last few days, wondering which indiscretion I would have to own up to this time. I breathed deeply and slid off my chair, preparing to face the music.

"What have you done now, Lexi?" my desk mate Rachael, smirked.

"Me?" I questioned, giving my best what-could-I-have-possibly-done look. Rachael threw her head back into a full throaty laugh. "Kate's pissed. I hope it was worth it," she said, fishing for a scoop on the latest office gossip.

"It's always worth it, Rach," I grinned and flicked my hair over my shoulder as I sauntered into Kate's office.

Kate Cole and I had known each other since university. Kate was a year ahead of me, and while we were not friends during our tenure, we were firm friends now. Kate was a force to be reckoned with, a strong woman with a keen business sense, amazing style and she saw the genius in the way I operated. She had built her PR and events company from the ground up, and the fact that Cole now had partnerships with offices on most continents of the world was testament to her genius and a key reason why I loved working with her. The other reason was that she welcomed my take-no-prisoner attitude, which had been too full on for my previous employer. He had claimed that I intimidated clients and thought I was some kind of placard toting feminist or lesbian. Lord knows, I couldn't just be a strong opinionated woman who knew her job.

I closed the door to Kate's stylish office behind me. It was a remarkably simple and sleek space, a reflection of her. She was not what you would call a 'girlie girl'. Kate loved sports and had very little tolerance for drama—a trait that had made her instantly appealing to me as both a boss and a friend.

"So... anything you want to tell me Lexi?" Kate paced the room as she deliberately breathed, a sure sign someone was in trouble. I still had no idea what I could have possibly done. Let's face it, the list of trouble I gotten myself into daily was long, so trying to narrow it down would have proven a challenge for anyone.

"You want to give me a hint Kate, or are we going to play mental charades?" I mused.

"Cut it out, Reed." Kate picked up the only file on her desk and came around to perch on one of the leather conversation chairs she used when she wanted to try and put her clients at ease. "I'm in a difficult situation here. You are forgetting I know you, and your history. Just help me understand if I need to hire a lawyer?" I took a long breath and settled into the seat opposite Kate. Clearly this was not going to be a five minute conversation.

"Kate, whatever it is, I am sure we can resolve it. Don't stress, OK?" She knew that this was not the first time I'd been threatened with legal action.

"Stacy is on stress leave. Effective immediately. She is claiming you called her crazy and have been tormenting her. She had a meltdown in front of our newest client yesterday afternoon during her presentation, calling us all a bunch of lying C-U-Next-Tuesdays."

I tried to stifle my laughter. "Are you shitting me Cole? That girl has been unhinged since the day she was hired," I exclaimed. "She is obsessive and overbearing. And when pray tell was I tormenting her? I haven't spoken to her in three months." While I had done lots of things which had the potential to lead to trouble, I was not going to be blamed for something I had had no part in.

"Lexi, I know the girl is certifiable, but I need to be one-hundred percent sure. I do not want an HR issue here..." Kate's pause for breath told me that she was really worried about this situation. "Did you tell someone she was on anxiety meds? She claims that you made some social media comments last month, on Facebook to be exact."

My head was pounding with fury. "What the fuck Kate? I didn't even know she was on meds. And if she is on meds, then clearly they aren't strong enough. As for my Facebook, you are on there – did you see any comments? I wasn't even in town last month. I was in New York, remember? I was too busy screwing and shopping to be on Facebook. What a fucking whore. She can't hold her own and she blames me? Get her on the phone. Let me confront her with these fucking accusations."

"Lexi, calm down, and for god's sake stop swearing. This is still an office." I relaxed a little as Kate clearly believed the truth of my story. "Look, I had my suspicions that the accusations were unfounded, but you have to understand my position. For now, she is on stress leave. It screws me over, as she was supposed to be going on this exchange program. I have a guy coming in from Texas tomorrow, and she was supposed to go there on Friday. I'm asking Rachael to go instead. I've already been on the phone all morning trying to sort this shit out."

My ears pricked up with interest. A guy from one of our partners in Texas? I hadn't had one of those before.

"Before you start getting all hot and heavy, he's off limits."

Off limits? Oh, Kate – don't you know that's like waving a red flag to a bull?

"I know you are a sucker for an accent, but I don't want to have to pick up the pieces of your sordid romp. Don't forget that this is my business, OK? Keep your hands, mouth and other body parts to yourself. We clear?" I was mentally rubbing my hands together in anticipation. "Lexi, I can see the cogs in your head turning. Seriously, I need to trust you on this one."

I widened my eyes in a show of false innocence. "Kate, you're making me out like I'm some insatiable fiend."

"Yeah, Yeah, you are so offended. Remember, I know you. Keep it in your pants, Reed," she said trying to force back a smile.

"Kate, Justin is on line one. The school has called and Sam is at the principal's office again," Jane's sugary sweet voice through the intercom burst into the office uninvited.

"Thanks Jane," Kate replied, taking a breath and clicking her finger over the flashing light. I waved silently and decided now was a good time to take my leave.

"Justin, I swear, this kid isn't going to make his next birthday," she said over the phone as I shut the door behind me.

I had spent a lot of time with Kate's four excitable, rambunctious boys. All of them were super competitive and sporty. The youngest, Sam, was the most challenging. He wasn't a bad kid, just very spirited, and he was the one I most identified with. Sometimes I wondered how Kate managed. I think the fact that her husband was so even-tempered was a calming influence. I really liked Justin. He was an uncomplicated guy. He worked hard, but when he came home it was all about his wife and his boys. He doted on Kate, allowing her to be the woman she was, and he wasn't threatened by her competitive ambition. She definitely wore the pants in that relationship, and he didn't really care. His tastes were simple – he loved his football, loved to have a beer and he loved his family. He was the yin to her yang. As sappy as it sounded, they had a perfect marriage and I hoped one day if I was ready to settle down—and that was a big if—I would find someone as honest as Justin.

"So. Did Kate tell you? I'm going to Texas," gushed Rachael as I returned to our cubicle. I could tell she had been holding onto her news, desperately wanting to share, but still trying to respect the chain of command and not making her announcement. However in true Rachael style she couldn't help herself.

"Stacey flipped out and went all psycho yesterday. Oh my god, so tragic, but her loss is my gain. I feel kinda bad, but at the same time I'm really excited. Is that wrong? Shit, I need to pack. Can you imagine the shopping over there? Everything is *big* in Texas." Her excitement was palpable, bordering on annoying, but it was on par for the course with Rachael.

"Rach, take a breath," I said, sitting down to my meticulously maintained desk and switching my monitor back on.

"I tell you this couldn't have come at a better time. Will is doing my head in. I went out for coffee the other night, and I had to check in. I told that man relax, I barely have enough time for you, as if I'm going to have time to cheat. He wouldn't listen. The break will be good for us. It will help me figure out what I want to do. Not that he's happy about it. Oh well, I'm so excited. Can you believe this shit? Oh my god, I swear, I haven't been this excited since my sister and I hit up Sydney."

Watching Rachael rush around in a frenzy, I couldn't help

but feel a twinge of jealousy. It would have been nice to jet off to a new city for six months, but I knew that Kate needed me here, and my role as a senior team member meant that I would be initiating this new guy into the office. I wondered what he looked like. I hadn't even asked Kate his name. The whole Stacey losing her shit drama threw me off my usual A-game. I needed details. I would need to take a walk down to visit Jane and see if I could pump her for intel. Kate's loyal PA could usually be persuaded to come up with the information.

"Lex. Are you even listening to me?" Rachael's voice rose an octave.

"Sorry Rach, I was distracted. What were you saying?"

"I asked if you had any good book suggestions for the plane? I wanted to load up my iPad with some trashy novels for the long journey. But, not any that are too sad. You know I'm a crier. Who knows, I might even find myself a new romance while I'm there."

I wasn't exceptionally close to Rachael. It's not that we weren't friends, we just moved in different circles. She was effervescent and full of life and always spoke like she was running a race. She was a really good person with a great heart, but we just didn't have a lot in common. I pushed my jealousy aside, realising that she was perfect for this new challenge. Those Texans were going to take one look at her massive personality and accept her as one of their own. I nodded in my silent resolve and gave her a big hug. "You're going to do great Rach, and if Will knows what's good for him, he'll realise what an arse he has been and jump on a plane and hopefully jump you too."

Rachael blushed. "Um. Gee. Thanks. Lexi. Um. Yeah."

What a freaking crazy morning. I swear there was so much to digest. I still needed to find out about our mysterious Mr Cowboy. I giggled. The things I could do with that rope. I wondered if he owned leather chaps and boots. This fantasy was getting hot. I could already feel the dull pleasure ache in my lower stomach and the slight moisture forming in my underwear. I wondered if Jane had a photo. I could totally Google him. I had to go get Jane a coffee. I'd learned from previous covert missions that she was a complete coffee addict and freer-flowing with information after she'd had her fix.

"Yummy. Is that for me?" Jane's saccharine voice squealed.

"Yep, I even got you one of the cookies you like." I held out the package and batted my eyelashes slightly. I had danced this dance before, and while Jane was good at her job, she wasn't the worldliest of creatures; she was naive and too trusting. This was going to be too easy. I could see the partially covered personnel file on her desk. "So Jane. I'm going to be showing the new guy around," I said pretending to look bored. "And I figured I'd quickly go through his file and see if there is anything I need to cover in his induction." Smooth Lexi, very smooth.

"Oh, I don't know Lexi, these files are kind of private. Kate would have my head, you know." Jane looked very uncomfortable with not giving me what I wanted, but she knew it would be breaking the rules to let me have access to a private HR file.

"Jane, do you think I would be asking if it wasn't OK with Kate?" I said, looking straight into her trusting brown eyes. "You saw me talking to her earlier didn't you? Remember when Justin called and I was in her office?" I marvelled at how easily the lies rolled off my tongue. I was a master of this game and Jane didn't even come close to being a worthy adversary.

"Well," Jane paused and looked from the coffee and biscuit

I was holding out to the files on her desk. "I guess if you have cleared it with Kate then it's OK."

Jackpot. I hoped there was some decent information in the file. I passed the delicious bribe over, and she hesitantly handed over the pristine manila folder in return, clearly having second thoughts until I gave her my award winning smile. Yep, entirely too easy. I should have been a spy or a con artist. Maybe Mr Cowboy and I can play on that fantasy as well? The list was endless.

I walked into one of the private meeting rooms. I wanted to do my recon without being disturbed and, let's face it, I was breaking company policy by accessing his personal details. While I was brazen, I wasn't stupid. I closed the door behind me and I settled into one of the comfortable chairs. As I opened the file, a sheet of paper slipped out. A small passport photo was paper-clipped to the side. *Wow cowboy, you're hot.* The photo was black and white, but I could tell his hair was dark and his eyes were so clear they were probably blue. He had a strong jawline with amazing bone structure that he could have been a model. The photo had obviously been taken later in the day with a light stubble accentuating his masculine features. His brows were furrowed and he had a distant, almost-forlorn look; like he was looking beyond the camera and straight into my soul. It was like he wasn't even trying to be sexy, yet it oozed out of every pore. Damn Kate and her no-fraternisation policy. I wondered what the outer edges of her definition would be. After getting a look at this new piece of talent, I was determined that I was going to find a loophole or at least skate to the edge of that line because 'Matthew Burns', whose name was printed across the top of his file, would be worth it.

Chapter 2

Well, Hello Cowboy!

MELBOURNE AIRPORT had always held such exciting memories for me; there was something about aviation fuel and jet noise that got me excited. The thrill of an impending trip or a loved one returning, what's not to love? And today, I was happily welcoming Matthew Burns into the Cole fold. I had slipped the file unnoticed back onto Jane's desk yesterday. She had been chatting on the phone to someone about the latest boy band who had captivated her interest, and I was sure she'd completely forgotten that I'd even taken the file. I quickly called Kate on my way out of the office, saying I thought it would be more personal to pick up Mr Burns rather than send a car or taxi, and while she had her reservations, she reluctantly agreed. "Don't make me regret this," were her parting words to me as I hung up the phone.

I had leapt out of bed this morning, throwing items of clothing all over my room in my haste to pick something suitable to wear. I finally settled on a fitted back shift dress and my red Steve Madden pumps. I finished the look with a slim-line jacket in the same red. I gazed into the mirror feeling a bit disconnected from the woman who stared back at me. I knew that I was not ugly, but no woman is ever really truly satisfied with herself. I think it's some weird glitch built into the second X chromosome. My big light brown eyes opened slightly wider as I studied my reflection. I had left my cascading mane of brunette curls loose, so they spilled onto my shoulders like an untamed waterfall.

My carefully manicured eyebrows arched back at me from my reflection. I had been told so many times I was beautiful, and yet I struggled to believe it. It was the chink in my armour, my dirty little secret. No one would ever believe I struggled with self-esteem. It's not what I projected. I glanced up and down at my body. I'd worked extra hard on my fitness over the last few months and the training and working out was showing results. My long arms travelled up the length of my thighs and over my firm butt. It was never enough. I would have to work harder. I mentally chastised myself – Lexi, you are a strong, successful, beautiful woman. Get over your hang ups. I fixed a smile on my face, and I walked out the door.

The flight had landed about an hour ago and people were starting to spill into the arrivals area where we were all corralled. I had flirted with the idea of holding up a sign with his name but decided it was too cheesy. Besides, those eyes – it's not like I could forget what he looked like. I spotted him as soon as he walked through the double doors. He was dressed in grey tailored pants, a light linen shirt, a matching tailored jacket and no tie. *Yum... I likey.* He was just less than six foot, and I could tell his body was toned even with his clothes on. His broad shoulders and chest filled his shirt and jacket nicely before his torso thinned to his lower abs and waist. His muscular arms flexing as he pushed the luggage trolley in front of him. "Mr Burns?" I questioned him as he came closer. He blinked in slight confusion at being approached and then a smooth grin spread across his face as he realised who I was. He had the same smattering of stubble across his face as he'd had in the photo. His clear blue eyes fixed on mine. "Hi, you must be Alexandra. Kate just sent me a text telling me you were going to meet me here." *Hmmm, what else had Kate told him?*

"Actually, it's Lexi. No one has called me Alexandra in years." I still felt like a naughty child whenever someone called me by my full name.

"Sorry, Lexi." His low gravelly voice caressed my name,

sending a shiver right to my core. "I'm Matt," he crooned, his smooth accent rolling off his tongue like morning dew off my windscreen. He held out his hand and gave me a firm but polite handshake.

"Well, Matt. You got everything? My car is just over here." I pulled my hand away from his warm grasp and spun on my heel, leading him to the parking garage walkway. He followed me, hanging slightly behind. I wasn't sure if it was because he was being polite, whether he didn't know where he was going, or maybe he was just checking out my arse. Either way, it wasn't long before we made it back to my car.

"Nice ride," he smirked, glancing at my silver Honda Civic as he lifted his suitcases off the trolley. Was he being sarcastic?

"Thanks, it does the job and it's easy to weave in and out of traffic." I cringed inwardly at my lame response. "So, Matt. Is this your first trip to Australia?" I steered the conversation back into my favour, while I helped him load his luggage into the back of my car.

"Yeah, it is actually, and I have to say my first impressions of this place are pretty good." Was he flirting? I couldn't quite work this one out.

Usually I could figure a guy out pretty quickly. Hell, most of the time I knew if I was going to sleep with him within the first five minutes of conversation, yet Mr Cowboy had me perplexed. He was standing at the driver's side door after I closed the hatch, having carefully stowed his suitcases away. "Um, unless you are going to drive, you are going to have to go around to the other side." I mused. He glanced inside at the steering wheel that was firmly in place on the wrong side of the car.

"Oh yeah, I completely forgot about that. I hear the water runs the opposite way down the drain down here too." I couldn't help but laugh at his innocent statement. I'd bet my new Mimco clutch, he'd be flushing the toilet the minute he got into his hotel to test his theory. He smiled as he sauntered passed me, moving to the passenger side and getting in.

The ride to the hotel was surprisingly smooth. He was easy to talk to and pretty funny as well. He was incredibly well mannered, and I was impressed by his knowledge of my home city. Chances are he'd probably read a traveller's guide book on the plane and was merely regurgitating it, but still it showed he made an effort. He was originally from Houston, Texas but went to College in Pittsburgh, Pennsylvania at Carnegie Mellon University. He loved his time in Pittsburgh and spent a few years working there after graduating, speaking fondly of the city that was his home during that time. "It's a lot like Melbourne in some ways," he explained. "It has amazing sports arenas and the city is full of diverse restaurants, born from the influx of ethnic migration back in the 1920s." He seemed passionate about knowing about a city's culture, and I could see his eyes light up when he spoke about Pittsburgh.

"Sounds like a place I'd probably like to visit," I mused.

"Oh, you have to go. I could give you a list of things to see and do, an absolute must is to have a Primantti's sandwich in the strip district. That sandwich will change your life," he grinned. I couldn't imagine any sandwich changing my life but I was willing to humour him.

The traffic was light so it didn't take too long to reach his hotel. He was only booked in until he found more suitable accommodation, hopefully an apartment he explained. He hated living out of a suitcase. I parked out front in the drop off zone and stepped out to help him with his bags.

"Lexi," he breathed. I glanced up at him. I had to tilt my chin back slightly to look him in the eyes, even with my killer Madden heels. "It was a pleasure meeting you and thank you for the ride. I'd love for you to meet me for dinner tonight and help me go through my schedule for tomorrow."

"Sure, I'll bring over all your induction paperwork if you like, and we can go over it together – saves you doing it in the morning." I couldn't peg this one. Was he asking me on a date? Was this business? What the hell? Was he gay? I must have been losing my edge. Perhaps I needed to up the ante tonight and try and work this one out. "I've got to stay back tonight to tie some loose ends in the office but I'll make it back by eight, OK?"

"Yes, we wouldn't want any loose ends," he smirked, and he turned as he headed into his hotel. OK that was fucking weird. I was going to be on edge for the rest of the day.

"Oi, Lexi," Anna giggled. I looked up from my computer screen to see her dark eyes staring at me over the wall partition.

"Hey Anna, you trolling for information to take back to your arsehole boss?" I smirked.

"Bitch, please, the arsehole is golfing today. I could be out to lunch for three hours and he'd be none the wiser. Now, if you're done assaulting that keyboard, grab your shit and let's go to lunch. It's Taco Tuesday," Anna retorted. I grabbed my bag and took my iPhone off my desk.

"So what's the goss, Anna? Any rumblings I should know about?" Anna worked at a rival events firm, so generally had to get a full pat down and provide a urine sample on arrival. Kate knew we were friends and had no issue with us 'networking' as long as I exercised discretion. Still, she insisted Anna leave her phone at reception and was accompanied to my desk by Jane, who eyed us impatiently as we left the office.

We made our way to the cosy little Mexican place down

the street and had barely been seated in our booth when Anna beamed, "I heard some shit went down in your office yesterday...." She left her sentence trail off deliberately. I knew it wouldn't be long before word was out of Stacey's undignified fall from grace. Still, Kate would be livid if I confirmed anything.

"Yeah, we landed that account you guys have had for the last five years," I glowed. "It was amazing how easy it was to convince Reece he was getting robbed over there at your place," I smiled as I signalled the waiter. I was hungry.

"*Ha*. You could argue the sky was green and convince people you were right – why do you think Kate has you as her right hand man? Arsehole would bring you across to our team in a heartbeat if he thought he stood a chance." We both smiled. "But, seriously, no work talk. I want to hear about Stacey. I heard she went all single white female. Apparently she was screaming and crying in a client meeting. Did she really call you all a bunch of C's?" Anna whispered in a hushed voice.

"What can I say? I evoke strong responses in people." I spat that out more curtly than I intended. I was annoyed that the crazy bitch was still on the payroll after all the shit she had pulled in recent months.

"A truer word never spoken." I heard it from over my shoulder. That familiar voice. I didn't need to turn around as I could see from Anna's wide-eyed expression and pen jaw that Matt was standing directly behind me. Oh, how I'd love for him to take me from behind, feel his strong arms reaching around and pulling me close to his strong athletic frame. "Mind if I join you ladies?" he continued, oblivious to my hardening nipples beneath my jacket.

"Sure," Anna sang out, almost a little too enthusiastically. "Lexi, are you going to introduce me to your friend?" she asked with a knowing smile.

"Matt, this is Anna – Anna, Matt. He's 'on loan' to us for six months and just got in from Texas this morning," I explained. I could see Anna mentally undressing him as she took his hand and shook it politely. He then sat down and flagged a waitress down for another menu.

"I thought you would have crashed by now. It's a long flight —aren't you jet lagged?" I queried Matt.

"Yeah, I am, but I find if I push through and sync with my new time zone I can usually beat it. I got bored in the room, so I thought I'd take a walk around, maybe get something to eat. I hate room service," he retorted.

"And yet of all the restaurants in this fine city of ours, you find yourself here, in the very one I'm at. Are you stalking me?" I purred.

A smile crept across his beautiful unshaven face. "Actually, I called the office when I realised I didn't have your cell number, and they told me where I might find you. But, if you prefer the stalking idea, we can go with that." I was slightly unnerved by his loaded retort. It had been a while since I had been challenged by man. This was going to be fun.

"Are you guys ready to order?" the impatient waitress tapped her foot.

"Sure, we'll have the fajitas, the chicken soft tacos and two pineapple Margaritas." Our order was always the same; I didn't even have to ask Anna. "Matt would you like a beer? There's plenty of food to share." I glanced over my menu at his clear blue eyes. Oh yes, I have played this game before Cowboy, anything you've got—I can do one better. Men were one thing I understood—I could play them like a well-strung guitar and when I got tired of them, I discarded them and went on to the new flavour of the month. I was not a whore, although I had been accused of being one so many times. So many people, men and women alike are threatened by a woman who is in touch with her sexuality and desire; it's just not socially acceptable for a woman to want a no-strings relationship. For me, it was the ultimate. I had no time for relationships, not real ones. I'd tried those earlier on before I worked out that I wasn't ready to play that game because all it got me was disappointment and a broken heart. I vowed that no man would ever control me like that again. I would hold the power – it would be about what I wanted and what I needed.

"Corona please, with lime." His silky voice didn't show any hint of annoyance. Our drinks arrived quickly and the conversation flowed as easily as it had earlier that morning. I could tell by the way Anna was looking at him that she would rather be devouring him than her lunch, but she wasn't as brazen as I was, so would bide her time. I cringed knowing the barrage of questions and requests that would surely follow.

"So Lexi, are we still on for dinner?" Matt asked, after he ate his first round of tacos. I watched Anna visibly deflate in the knowledge that we would spending the evening together. Anna was beautiful and smart, but she knew she couldn't compete with me when it came to men—she was too nice. I generally backed off when I knew one of my friends was interested in a guy as this was just sport to me, but to them an opportunity for happiness. I wasn't completely callous and unscrupulous. Matt was different though. I couldn't place what it was, but I felt compelled to play this out. *Sorry Anna—I can't yield, not this time.*

"Yes, of course. I was actually wondering if you would like a home-cooked meal. I figured it would be easier to discuss business in a more comfortable setting and will give me time to fully brief you for tomorrow's staff meeting." *More like fully debrief you and get down to business,* I silently corrected in my head.

"Home cooked meal sounds wonderful, it's been a while." The smile creeping across his face lit up his features.

"Great, I'll pick you up at eight." Home field advantage—this was going to be a cake walk.

"Well ladies, thank you for lunch. I'm afraid the jetlag is kicking my ass right now though, so I think it's best I head off and try and get some shut eye."

"Well it was so nice to meet you Matt, hopefully I will see you again soon?" There was still hope hanging in Anna's voice.

Matt smiled as he met her eyes, "I look forward to it." He turned his gaze to mine. "See you tonight, at eight." He took my iPhone from the table and programmed his number in. "Just in case something comes up," he said, placing my phone back down before making his exit.

Anna glowered at me, and I knew how the rest of this conversation was going to go. I took a deep breath, readying myself for Anna's verbal assault when the waitress brought us the bill. 'Paid in full' was scrawled across the receipt. We stared at each other silently. That sneaky bastard.

ABOUT THE AUTHOR

T Gephart is an indie author from Melbourne, Australia.
T's approach to life has been somewhat unconventional. Rather
than going to University, she jumped on a plane to Los Ange-
les, USA in search of adventure. While this first trip left her
somewhat underwhelmed and largely depleted of funds it
fueled her appetite for travel and life experience.
With a rather eclectic resume, which reads more like the fiction
she writes than an actual employment history, T struggled to
find her niche in the world.

While on a subsequent trip the United States in 1999, T met
and married her husband. Their whirlwind courtship and
interesting impromptu convenience store wedding set the tone
for their life together, which is anything but ordinary. They
have lived in Louisiana, Guam and Australia and have travelled
extensively throughout the US. T has two beautiful young children and one four legged child, Woodley, the wonder dog.

An avid reader, T became increasingly frustrated by the lack of
strong female characters in the books she was reading. She
wanted to read about a woman she could identify with,
someone strong, independent and confident who didn't lack
femininity. Out of this need, she decided to pen her first book,
A Twist of Fate. She enjoyed the process so much that when it
was over she couldn't let it go.

T loves to travel, laugh and surround herself with colourful characters. This inevitably spills into her writing and makes for an interesting journey - she is well and truly enjoying the ride!

Frustrated by the lack of strong female characters in the current fiction, T was reading she set herself the challenge to write something that was interesting, compelling and yet easy enough to read that was still enjoyable. Pulling from her own past "colourful" experiences and the amazing personalities she has surrounded herself with, she had no shortage of inspiration. With a strong slant on erotic fiction, her core characters are empowered women who don't have to sacrifice their femininity.

Based on her life experiences, T has plenty of material for her books and has a wealth of ideas to keep you all enthralled.

For more on T -
Website - www.tgephart.com
FaceBook - www.facebook.com/tgephartauthor

BOOKS BY THIS AUTHOR

The Lexi Series

Lexi

A Twist of Fate

Twisted Views: Fate's Companion

A Leap of Faith

A Time for Hope

The Power Station Series

High Strung

Crash Ride

Back Stage

The Black Addiction Series

Slide

Sticks

Stand

#1 Series

#1 Crush

#1 Player

#1 Rival

#1 Lie

#1 Muse

#1 Love

Collision Series
Train Wreck

Car Crash

Standalones
The Fall

One-Night Stand-In

www.ingramcontent.com/pod-product-compliance
Lightning Source LLC
Chambersburg PA
CBHW020619120726
47905CB00003B/855